How I Fell in Love with a Librarian

and Lived to Tell About it

Rhett Ellis

Fiction/Religion

ISBN 0-9670631-4-0

For Cole

Thanks to Audrey, Dayton, and Jo Ann Cook, and Tina Nabors, for your help and friendship.

One

When I walked into the Clegmore Public Library on Wednesday, February 5 of last year, I was not expecting to see the most beautiful woman in the entire world, nay, the most beautiful creature in all existence, standing behind the circulation desk, but I did, and I still haven't fully recovered from the shock. It's not that I accepted the stereotype of the librarian—hair in a bun, spectacles on a chain about her neck, dark dress, austere manner, etc. It's just that in Clegmore, Alabama one never expects to see a new face, much less the face of the most beautiful woman in the whole universe.

My name is Robert Chesterfield Smith, and I turn thirty seven this year. I have brown hair, brown eyes, and an altogether average physique. To look at me is to see nothing special. I am a preacher, and the only thing about me that you might find interesting (or strange) is: I started preaching when I was a fifteen year old Sunday School student, and I could always address a crowd of any size, from a senior citizen's living room prayer circle to a young people's rally at a football stadium, with perfect confidence and complete ease, but upon meeting a pretty woman, I could never so much as utter a coherent sentence without my voice cracking, my palms sweating, my eyes blinking, and my knees shaking.

I preach three times a week at the Shiloh Baptist Church on the corner of Eighth and McKay on the southeast side of town, and I am constantly searching for illustrative material—stories, facts, and quotes to help liven up the points of my sermons—and the library is the best place to search.

Inez Cunningham, Clegmore's librarian since around the time that Eisenhower took office until November of year before last, was, until she had her stroke, the most helpful person I ever met. I could walk into the library at fifteen minutes before closing time on a Saturday afternoon, and tell her I needed some material for a sermon about Moses in Pharaoh's Court for Sunday Morning; three minutes later, I would see, as if they had materialized from the air, a stack of books on Nile Valley history and copies of National Geographic with articles on King Tut's treasures and the building of the pyramids.

"Thanks for the books, Mrs. Cunningham," I would say, "but you know I can't take the magazines home. It's against the rules."

"And who do you think made the rules for this library?" she would ask. "I did, of course, and I get to say who breaks them."

The Clegmore Library got Internet access seven years ago, but given a choice between the World Wide Web and Mrs. Cunningham, I chose Mrs. Cunningham for information every time.

Mrs. Cunningham, a large woman who got out of breath when she over-exerted herself, which she did at least once a day, was reaching up to a top shelf in the fiction department to get a book between Hawthorne and Hemmingway (no one ever knew for sure which book) when she had her stroke. She fell backward and hit her head against the opposite shelf in the area between Wodehouse and Woolf, and with her right foot, which had begun to shake uncontrollably, she kicked over all the books on the bottom shelf between King and Lewis.

Her assistant called 911, and Mr. Lowelle, a widower and retiree who spent part of most afternoons reading the newspapers at the library, called me on his mobile phone. He thought a minister should be on the scene, and as it happened, at the very moment that Mrs. Cunnigham fell, he was reading the announcements page of the *Clegmore Progressive*, and on the page was a mention of my church's upcoming Thanksgiving

Dinner with the Shiloh Baptist Church's office phone number.

I got in my car, rushed to the library, and arrived after the first police cruiser but before the ambulance. I ran inside after the policeman, but neither I nor the officer, who stepped into the library just before I did, saw anything unusual. We stood in place and looked about until we heard Mr. Lowelle call out: "She's over here."

I followed the officer past the non-fiction area, turned down the aisle before the one where Mrs. Cunningham lay, and approached her with caution. Her right hand was trembling, and her hair, which was always styled to perfection and sprayed in place, was disheveled and messy.

The assistant, one of the girls from the high school who came in each afternoon to help with the tedious work, was holding Mrs. Cunningham in her arms, and Mr. Lowelle was fanning her face with the *Clegmore Progressive's* sports section.

"Let her lie down," the officer said. "The ambulance is pulling up outside."

I prayed for Mrs. Cunningham, but since we all have to go sooner or later, I did not pray that her life would be spared so much as I prayed that she would not have to suffer too much or too long. I guess my prayer was answered because she died three hours later in the Intensive Care unit at the Clegmore Community Hospital. I tried to comfort her children, who had arrived by that time, but I was too tearful myself to help them very much.

The library closed for the rest of the week. Her funeral was held at the Clegmore First Presbyterian Church on Saturday, and on Sunday, the *Clegmore Progressive* ran a front page article on Mrs. Cunningham's life and contributions to the community.

On Monday morning the city council met to discuss what should be done to replace her, and having made all my hospital visits that morning and having nothing else to do, I attended.

"We'll never replace Mrs. Cunningham," Mayor Monty

Jordan, owner of Jordan's Office Supply, said after everyone was seated.

"Nope, we never will," Council Member Linda Delchamp, a full time beautician, agreed.

After a long pause, by which the council members silently expressed their agreement that Mrs. Cunningham could never be replaced and that this meeting was not intended to show any disrespect to her memory, Langston Long, owner of Long's Motor Company, said: "And maybe we shouldn't try. People get most of what they need to know from the Internet these days. The library is a big expense, and maybe it's time to think about letting it go."

I couldn't believe my ears. I would have said something immediately, but the designated time for questions or comments from the general public had not come.

Pete Wycliffe, full time accountant, countered, "We can't do that. I'd vote to let just about anything else go, the sports complex or even the city park, before I'd vote to let the library go."

"Well, why not?" Langston Long shot right back. "Who needs it? It's nothing but a drain on the town's finances and this city needs a lot of fixing up."

Langston was an aggressive old salesman, and Pete, a young C.P.A., was taken aback and said nothing at first, but Linda Delchamp, who never liked Langston Long and made no secret of it, said: "Of course we're not letting the library go. There's not another public library for thirty miles in every direction, and without it, this town and the whole west end of this county would, in my opinion, take a big step backwards both educationally and culturally."

I've seen Linda in the library many times, but I've never seen her checking out books that are educational or cultural unless by educational she meant mysteries and by cultural she meant romances. Still, she had a point.

"I agree with Linda," Mayor Jordan said.

"So do I," agreed Marie Wilton, a doctor's widow who probably has more education and culture than anyone in Clegmore. "And I move that we assign the Library Board the task of searching for Mrs. Cunningham's successor as soon as possible."

Langston Long rolled his eyes, shook his head, and sighed because he knew he was all alone on the idea of discontinuing support for the library.

"I second the motion," Pete Wycliffe said.

"Any discussion?" Mayor Jordan asked.

None of the council members spoke.

"Any questions or comments from those in attendance?" the mayor asked.

I considered voicing my agreement for Marie Wilton's motion, but with four of the five council members obviously ready to vote in favor of it, I thought it unnecessary to do so. Langston Long, not wanting to be thought the obstinate one, abstained from voting, and it carried four to zero.

Library Board member Carol Albritton attends Shiloh church every Sunday morning. I spoke with her a week after the meeting, and she said the board had run an ad on the American Library Association's website but did not expect to make much progress in its search for Mrs. Cunningham's replacement until after the new year, and that for now, it had hired the librarian from Clegmore High to come in each afternoon and on weekends to open the library and make sure the assistants kept it as orderly as possible.

I was used to visiting the library any old time I wanted during weekdays, but for the next two months I had to make an effort to get there between three and five in the afternoon, and I had to do all my own research. The library board searched diligently, and Carol kept me posted on its progress. Around the middle of January, the board conducted interviews, and a week later announced that it had found a new librarian. Carol said the board felt good about its choice. I asked her the new librarian's name, but she said she could not give out any information until an updated job description had been created and a new contract had been written.

I forgot about the matter until Wednesday, February 5, and that brings us back to where we started. I woke up that morning at seven, had a left over square of lasagna for breakfast, took a shower, and put on a brown button down shirt and khaki pants— plain clothes for what I thought would be a plain day. At eight o' clock, while on my way to the church office, I drove past the library and noticed a number of cars in its parking lot, most notably Ben Dunning's blue Nissan pickup.

Ben is my best friend and the *Clegmore Progressive's* only full time reporter. His presence implied that there must have been something newsworthy to see. I turned around, wheeled my forest green Toyota back into the parking lot, and pulled it into the space beside Ben's truck.

When I opened my car's door, the air felt cooler than it had when I left the house, and I regretted not bringing a jacket. I crossed my arms and hurried to the library's main entrance. I pushed open the door, glanced at the desk, and stopped dead in my tracks.

Standing behind the circulation desk was a young woman with green eyes. At first I saw nothing but her eyes, and they struck me as possessing more beauty than Helen of Troy had from head to toe. Her eyes seemed to smile at everyone and to sparkle in the sunlight that was coming in through the windows on the library's east side.

If merely pretty girls had always made me nervous, you can imagine how I felt gazing upon a woman whose appearance exuded a glory greater than any of the treasures I had seen in the Ancient China issue of National Geographic. My jaw dropped, and I turned to walk right back out the door, but Ben Dunning saw me and said, "Rob, come on over and meet Miss Findley."

Although Ben talks with a southern accent, he is clear in

what he says, and he definitely said "miss" and that implied she was single. I glanced at her left hand and saw no ring.

"Myra Findley," Ben said, "Meet Robert Smith, pastor at the Shiloh Baptist Church. Most people call him Brother Rob. Rob, meet Myra Findley."

"Hi, Brother Rob," Myra Findley said as she extended her hand for a shake. Her voice sounded like music. One Christmas when several local choirs united to sing *The Messiah*, Mrs. Cunningham put me onto an article about the process by which Handel wrote it. It didn't take him long to complete *The Messiah*, the article said, because it was as if he heard the choirs of heaven singing the music. When Myra Findley spoke I felt like Handel because her voice sounded perfectly celestial.

I tried to say "Hi," but what came out of my mouth was something more like "Hu" or "Heh," I think. It's hard to say exactly what I said because I didn't hear myself.

I reached out to shake her hand, and the moment our hands touched, I felt electricity run out of her fingertips. The volts coursed up my arm and spread all over me.

I turned and rushed toward the reference section, and fortunately Miss Findley was so busy meeting people and fielding questions from Ben for his upcoming article "Clegmore Welcomes New Librarian" that she didn't seem to notice my abrupt self removal.

From behind the shelves of the reference section, I glanced over the tops of and between the gaps in the rows of books. Every time I gazed at her, I felt waves of wonder mixed with nervousness wash through my being.

One by one, the "welcome committee" began to clear out, and I realized that I would soon be the only patron in the library, all alone with Myra Findley, and the idea terrified me. I just wasn't up to it.

I would have exited immediately but doing so would have required walking past the desk, and if someone stopped me to talk, I would have been trapped and unable to move my mouth; so I waited. Sure enough, after awhile everybody left, and there we were, just the two of us.

At first it seemed that she had forgotten that I was there, and I was thinking about putting my head down and exiting as fast as I could without making eye contact as I passed her desk, but before I had a chance, she said: "May I help you with something?"

My heart fell into my stomach, and my mind raced to find words, but all I could say was, "Uh," which, I suppose, sounded more like a "No" than a "Yes" to her because she said: "Okay, but if you need any help, just let me know."

I continued to scamper behind the shelves until she left her desk and stepped into the ladies' room. The moment the door closed behind her, I made a dash for the exit. I got in my car, cranked it, and drove toward Shiloh Baptist Church, but all I could think about as I drove was the fact that, though I did not believe in love at first sight, there was a better than good chance that I had just fallen in love with Myra Findley and that I was going to have to do something to win her love in return, even if it killed me.

Two

I arrived at the office late. The little red light on the answering machine was flashing, and I had to return several phone calls, but there was no bad news and nothing major to attend, just routine questions. I brought in the mail, thumbed through it, tossed most of it in the trash, and placed the one item that was not junk mail on my desk, a bill to be directed to the attention of the church treasurer.

Suddenly I had an idea: I would go talk with Ben at the *Progressive.* I didn't want to show up in his office without a good reason so I picked up the church calendar and searched for an excuse to visit the newspaper. The church's next special event was the annual Valentine's banquet. The event had never been publicized throughout the community, but this year the whole town would know about it. I jotted down the date and time.

Ben is a large man with blonde hair and a smile that is usually warm but becomes a smirk rather often, and he likes to talk. He and I attended all twelve years of school together, and he has been my best friend since third grade, but our lives could not be more different. He got married soon after high school, and he and his wife had their first child before they finished college.

Ben's daughter was graduating from Clegmore High in the spring, and that seemed impossible to me. I couldn't imagine what marriage was like, much less having kids, but if I could talk casually to anybody, it would be Ben.

I dropped the announcement off at the front desk with Winnie Dunning, Ben's mom. I waved at Ben's father, John

Dunning, publisher and chief editor of the *Clegmore Progressive*, who was sitting behind his office's glass partition, talking on the phone. He waved back, and I walked over to Ben's office and knocked on his door.

Wood, not glass, served as walls for Ben's office because, as he put it, he needed at least a little bit of privacy from his parents.

He asked: "Who's there?"

"It's me, Rob." I said.

"Come on in, Rob, and have a seat. Got any news?"

I sat down in the brown leather chair that faced his desk.

"Nah, not really," I said. "I just dropped off an announcement about our Valentine's banquet, and I thought I'd stop by and chat with you for awhile. How've you been doing?"

"Fine. It's been a slow news week, but let's face it, this town hasn't had a fast news week since a hundred years ago when it was founded."

I tried to seem relaxed. "Well, how do you think the new librarian's going to do?" I asked, trying to sound as casual as I possibly could.

"Don't know. It's going to be hard to replace Mrs. Cunningham." Ben said. "But this new girl just got her master's from Auburn, and she's looking to update the way the library does business, and it certainly could use it, no disrespect to Mrs. Cunningham. The Clegmore Library is still stamping cards on book checkouts. It's time to get a computer system and scan 'em and send 'em out the way the big libraries do. The library got in early on the Internet, but it hasn't made any progress since then."

"You say she just got her master's from Auburn? How old is she?"

"Twenty-four years old," Ben said.

Being careful not to move my lips, I calculated our age difference. She was, give or take, about twelve years younger than me.

"I've never seen her around here," I said. "Does she have family in the area?"

"None that I know of. Her family is from the Huntsville

area. Why do you ask about her? You're not interested, are you?"

In a town like Clegmore, word spreads fast. No, that's an understatement. Word spreads very fast. The people of Clegmore spread rumors faster than a tornado spreads debris, and I knew I'd better be careful lest words of my intentions reached her ears before I was ready to speak them myself so I played stupid.

"Huh? What do you mean?"

"You know. Are you interested in going out with her?" Ben asked.

"Your reporter's instinct makes you too suspicious. I'm one of the library's most active customers, you know."

"Okay, I won't give you a hard time, then."

I tried to seem relaxed again, chuckled, leaned back in the chair, and changed the topic: "Well, basketball season is about to wind down. How's the high school team looking this year?"

Ben's favorite part of his job is covering sports, and he is always happy to offer an opinion on the subject. He told his predictions for the last part of the season, which weren't optimistic, and the conversation moved on.

I stayed a few more minutes, told him I was sorry I had to be going, and said goodbye.

That afternoon I had three visits to make at the community hospital—an elderly lady in for a heart cath, an elderly gentleman with pneumonia, and a middle-aged woman recovering from an appendectomy.

I tried to move through the visits in my usual manner, asking the questions I ordinarily ask, saying the things I ordinarily say to try to comfort people during hard times, but each patient brought up the new librarian.

I was already going out of my mind with thoughts of Myra Findley, and it seemed that the only subject anyone wanted to talk about was her. This did not help matters.

For lunch, I drove to Grandma's Kitchen, a cafe to the north of Clegmore, which serves country food. I ordered the lunch special: ham, squash, lima beans, cornbread, cake, and tea, and as I ate I told myself that I must not be a coward, that I must return to the library and do my best to make the acquaintance of Myra Findley, come what may. If I had acted cowardly that morning it had been because I was neither expecting nor prepared to deal with love at first sight, or infatuation, or whatever it was.

Faith Petree, my favorite waitress because she always remembers that I like lemon with my tea and butter with my cornbread and never has to ask, sat down on the bench on the opposite side of the table and said, "You okay? You look like you got something heavy on your mind."

"Oh, I'm fine. You know how it is dealing with people." I tried to keep it vague.

"Yeah, tell me about it. I need to drag my old man down to your church some day so you can straighten him out. I think he's gettin' worse every year." She laughed, topped off my tea, and disappeared into the back of the restaurant.

After lunch, I drove straight to the library, stopping only at Jake's Pack'n'Save to buy some breath mints. When I touched the library door's brass handle, I felt something worse than butterflies in my stomach. It was more like a swarm of hornets.

Steady, I told myself, *you'll not be attempting anything but a good introduction, nothing to get upset about.*

I opened the door, stepped inside, and breathed in that library smell. She was not at the front desk. *Probably in back,* I thought. Fortunately I had a legitimate reason to visit the library that afternoon—preparation for the Wednesday night prayer service's Bible study.

The topic was to be: *Building Our House on the Rock instead of the Sand: Standing on the Words of Christ against the Storms of Life.*

I searched the card catalogue for books on weather, beaches, construction, and rock formations, and as I searched, I felt her enter the room. My back was to the circulation desk, and I did not see so much as a shadow, but somehow I knew that if I turned around I would see her standing there.

A second later, she confirmed what I sensed by asking: "May I help you find something?"

Finding a book involved no personal interaction of any depth so I felt somewhat comfortable when I turned and answered: "I'm looking for books on weather, beaches, construction, and rocks."

Standing immediately before her, waiting for her to answer, I was able to take my first full gaze at her face. To frame her green eyes, she had dark hair and fair skin. She had a slender waist, fine features, and a long, graceful neck. Her physique was that of a tall, slim woman, but she had feminine hips and looked somewhat athletic.

"Interesting combination," she said as she reached down and pulled one of the drawers from the card catalogue. "I'm new here, but I think I know where to start."

"Yes, I know," I said.

"You know what?" she asked, looking up.

"I know you're new here. We met this morning."

She glanced at me again.

"Oh yes, I'm sorry." she said. "There have been so many new faces today. Your name started with an *R*, right?"

"Right," I managed to say with much effort while I thought: *No way! The most beautiful woman in the world knows the first letter of my name. No way!*

"And it is?"

"And *what* is?" I asked.

"What is your name?"

"Oh, it's Robert Smith."

"You're a minister, right?"

"Yes," I said. I was feeling so nervous that just the one syllable required a great deal of exertion. Not only did the most beautiful woman in the world know my name, she knew my vocation.

"Well, are you building a cottage at Gulf Shores or research-ing for a sermon?" she asked.

"Sermon," I said. "Wednesday night Bible study. Do you go to church?"

"Not in a long time." she said, and her tone of voice implied that I should not ask any further questions about the subject.

"Ah, here's one for you." She placed the wooden drawer on a table, stepped around a shelf, shuffled through some books, and returned a minute later holding a large, full color atlas of the earth that covered beaches, rock formations, and weather. Three subjects down with one book and only one more subject to go— certainly not as fast as Mrs. Cunningham, but for her first day on the job, not half bad. I was impressed.

"What about construction?" I asked.

"Oh, I'm sure there are several books on that subject in the card catalogue. You should have no trouble finding them," she said as she handed me the drawer labeled *bur-cre* and walked back behind the desk. "If you can't find them, just let me know, and I'll help."

Mrs. Cunningham would have never responded so coldly to a request for help finding a book, and at first it seemed that Miss Myra Findley was being rude, but the expression on her face told me that her response was not rude, that it was quite normal, that librarians weren't supposed to do *everything* for their patrons. Mrs. Cunningham had been spoiling me for years, and I would have to get over it and do my own research from now on, simple as that.

Finding the books did not take long, and I chose one titled *America's Historic Lighthouses* because it fit well with the evening's lesson and because it had the most pictures. Contrary to what one would think, for public speakers, books with lots of pictures can be more helpful than books with lots of words because it is much easier to describe pictures than to repeat words.

As she stamped the books, I said, "Thanks," and as I exited

20

the library, I said, "Take care."

I knew that if I said much more it would have seemed forced and awkward. I had already spoken more to her than I thought I could, and I did not want to push it. As the door closed behind me, I determined that I would not return to the library except when I had a legitimate need to do so because doing otherwise would create awkwardness, and it would not be fair to the new librarian. A true gentleman must never invade a lady's personal space.

Three

Every Wednesday evening, Shiloh Baptist Church holds Bible study for all ages, and while the children and youth meet with their leaders in their age specific groups, I lead the adult group. Despite the helpful books, I felt unprepared and too rattled to lead the study, and it seemed to me that my presentation of the lesson was lacking in several areas. A number of those in attendance, however, said I spoke with more enthusiasm than usual, and I thanked them for the compliment.

I passed the bill that had arrived that morning to the treasurer, and she asked if I were feeling okay. I told her I was, but she seemed skeptical. After everyone left the church, I turned off the lights, locked up, and started toward home. As I drove past the library I noticed that the lights were on, and that Myra Findley's car was parked in the side parking lot.

Wow, I thought, *it's nearly ten o'clock. She must be totally dedicated to her job. Surely she's one of those near perfect people with whom someone like me should not be preoccupied.*

I thought back to my afternoon encounter with her, especially the way she made me do my own research. Yes, she was the perfect picture of strength, self-confidence, poise, grace and elegant beauty. Myra Findley was definitely out of my league.

Being a bachelor with a great deal of flexibility in my schedule, for many years I had done my grocery shopping at night when the lines at the registers tended to be short. I needed a few items—cereal, milk, frozen chicken pot pies, and soap—so I stopped at the Food Fiesta and went inside.

I removed a shopping cart from the cart corral, but one of its wheels wouldn't turn so I pushed it to the side and reached for another. As I was removing the second cart, I heard the sound of car tires screeching to a halt. I looked out the plate glass window and thought I saw Myra Findley's car, a maroon and white Buick, but the slump-shouldered woman who opened the driver's side door and got out could not have been her.

From a distance, I could see only the woman's shape and overall demeanor. She took short steps but moved fast, and as she walked, she kept running her fingers through her hair, which even from a distance I could tell was a complete mess. There was something so quirky about the way the woman moved that I could not take my eyes off her as she crossed the parking lot and walked through the automatic door.

When she stepped inside the store, I glanced at her face. At first I did not recognize her, but when she glanced back, to my great shock and amazement, I realized that she *was* Myra Findley. I blinked. No, I told myself, she could not have been Myra Findley, but, yes, she was Myra Findley, the most beautiful woman in the entire world—or was she?

She did not recognize me as she brushed past, grabbed the cart with the bad wheel, and pushed it toward the fruits and vegetables section.

I could not help following after her, but I did so at a distance. She was mumbling something under her breath so I moved to within hearing distance.

She picked up an apple and mumbled:

Apple, apple,
Red, red, red,
There are no apples
In my head.

That was good to hear, but I wasn't sure I believed it. As she

24

turned the corner, she stopped over a wide crack in the tile and said:

Mean old crack,
Tryin' to throw me off track,
Make me break my back,
And spend a year in a shack,
With my neck outta whack,
Oh look, the lettuce rack!

She passed a tall man at the lettuce rack and mumbled in such a way that he could not hear, and I could hear only because I was listening intently and watching the movement of her lips:

If we eat our lettuce,
The germs won't get us.

Myra Findley, I realized, was not the most beautiful woman in the world. She wasn't even in contention for the position. Whatever magical feelings I had felt that morning had evaporated, but strangely I still felt interested in her in some way. She seemed like someone who needed help, and helping is what I do for a living. Now that her aura had vanished, I felt I could talk to her.

She pulled down the first aisle, stopped in front of the shaving supplies, and said:

I'll need some lotion
To shave my legs.
They keep me in motion.

"Myra," I said, and she let out a little yelp and said.

If you're a salesman, don't be a worry.

I've already bought, and I'm in a hurry.

"Bought what?" I asked, hoping she would relax and stop making rhymes, but she replied:

If you're a thief, leave me alone.
I don't have nothing so I'll be gone.

With that, she pushed her shopping cart, which was rattling and whining because of the bad wheel, as fast as she could down the aisle and turned it sharply. I decided to keep a great distance as I backed my cart out of the personal items aisle and moved parallel to her on the opposite side of the store. She moved past the registers as I moved past the meat department. She turned into frozen foods, and so did I, but I went down the opposite side of the open top ice cream freezer that ran down the center of the aisle.

When we drew close, I looked away, hoping to avoid rousing her suspicions, but she looked right at me and said:

There you are, I know your face.
You can't fool me, you're that...

She paused, apparently stuck.
"Minister," I said. "I'm the minister you met this morning."
"No, no, no, I know your face. You're..."
She paused again.
"The salesman?" I asked.
"No, your face, you're..."
"The thief?" I asked.
She didn't answer immediately so I waited. She moved her lips, and after a minute or so, she said:

I know your face,

26

You want to have a shopping cart race.

At least it rhymed. In seminary I had taken several psychology classes, and I had read about her pattern of behavior. I began to worry for her safety, and I considered calling the police to see if they could keep her from driving, but I had a feeling that she had her own way of dealing with her problem and would be just fine.

I pushed my cart away and said, "Have a nice evening, Miss Findley," but she did not seem to hear me.

I circled back around the ice cream freezer and started my shopping. I passed by her once more, and she seemed to notice me, but she turned her face away and mumbled something I could not interpret.

After I checked out, I placed my items in my car's trunk, got in the driver's seat, and watched for her to exit. Through the store's glass front, I could see her as she stood at the register. She looked down at the floor and shifted her weight from foot to foot as she waited for the clerk to ring up her groceries. She paid with cash, and when the clerk returned her change, she snatched it out of his hand, stuffed it into her purse, and looked around the store as if to make sure that no one had seen.

She had bought a full cart load of groceries, and as she toiled to get the cart over the automatic door's seal and across the less than smooth parking lot, she made strange faces and moved her lips rapidly.

With much haste, she transferred the items from the cart to her car's front seat, climbed in beside them, peeled out of the parking lot and drove away.

A part of me wanted to follow her to make sure she got home okay, but that seemed invasive, and I decided against it. I drove to my house—a square, two bedroom, one bath, one story, brick cottage on Eighth Avenue—and unloaded the items from the store.

After I put everything away, I sat down on the couch, reclined, and turned on the TV. I tried to take in some of the late night comedians, but my mind kept going over the events of the day. How could I have thought that Myra Findley was the most beautiful woman in the world? She wasn't even pretty. Had I experienced temporary insanity? Was the poise and grace that I thought I had seen merely stiffness on her part due to excessive nervousness, or worse, had I seen a figment of my own imagination?

I rolled the questions over and over in my mind until my eyelids got too heavy to hold up, and I went to bed. If I dreamed about her I don't remember it, but when I woke up the next morning I felt better.

Four

When I woke up the next morning, I microwaved some water, poured some instant coffee, drank it, dressed and drove to the church. I kept a small collection of books on the shelves in my office, and I searched through it until I found my old abnormal psychology text book from seminary, took it down, and flipped through its pages. There were at least three disorders that Myra Findley might have been suffering—or maybe it was a combination of all of them or maybe just two of them. Realizing I was no expert, I did not bother to speculate too much. The best thing for her would be to get help if she was not receiving it already.

I had the excuse of needing to look up some illustrations for Sunday morning's sermon so I left the office and drove to the library. I was not sure how I would approach the poor, tortured young woman, and I certainly was not sure how I would work in a suggestion that she see Dr. Sal Hernandez, the psychiatrist from Montgomery who visited our local hospital once a week, but when I pushed open the door to the library's main entrance, all my uncertainties vanished, for standing beside a row of shelves was the most beautiful woman in the world, Myra Findley. She appeared exactly as she had the previous morning. She looked perfect, and that seemed only natural.

I turned to my right, walked between two shelves, lowered my head, and looked through the books as I watched her through the corner of my eye. She helped an elderly couple find books in the fiction section, and her entire manner exuded warmth, politeness, and genuine care. She showed a young woman who attended the junior college on the other end of the county how to look up periodical references for a term paper. When she glanced out the window and saw a green van park in the handicap space, she went outside and helped a middle-aged man get out of his vehicle and she pushed his wheelchair onto the concrete in front of the library.

I recognized the man in the wheelchair. I knew he liked to maintain his independence, and he did not like to receive help from anyone, but Myra had managed to help him without condescending or showing pity in any way. From the moment she approached, he must have sensed that she respected him because he gladly allowed her to help and thanked her before she walked back inside.

Wow, what a lady! I should have felt confused, but I only felt joy. Whatever I had seen the previous evening had been an illusion, surely that was all. Maybe she had been a little stressed after her first day on the job, or maybe she had been joking and I had failed to pick up on it, but she absolutely could not have been suffering anything like a psychological abnormality. If I had witnessed beauty the previous morning, what I then saw was something better than beauty. There was a sweetness about her eyes that I could not have described if I had known the vocabulary of every language on earth—only the language of angels could have done it justice.

At last she approached me.

"Good morning," she said, and as she spoke, she smiled, and it seemed that her perfect white teeth glowed with their own light. For a second I got lost in her smile, and I could not think of anything to say.

"May I help you with something?" she asked, and her voice was soothing like a mountain stream splashing over pebbles.

"Priorities," I said. "I'm doing a series of sermons on the subject of priorities. We must learn to love people more than we love material things. People must be our priority."

"Pretty broad subject," she said, "so there should be plenty of material. Follow me."

Like a dog on a chain, I followed her to the card catalogue.

She opened a drawer, flipped through the cards and said: "Here's one for a short biography of Florence Nightingale. She was a lady who had her priorities in order, don't you think?"

"Yes, yes," I said, feeling every bit as stupid as I must have sounded to her.

She wrote down a number and pulled out another drawer.

"Would you care to sprinkle in some poetry by Alfred Lord Tennyson—better to have loved and lost than never to have loved and all that, you know."

"Yes, Alfred Lord Tennyson," I repeated, not fully aware of what I was saying.

"*A History of Christian Missions*," she said. "How does that grab you for a title on making people a priority? It's in the religion section."

"I've looked through that one before," I said. "Yes, a good book."

"Excellent. These should be enough to get you started, and if you need additional assistance, don't hesitate to ask."

Her tone of voice, however, said that she had given me all the assistance I deserved and that I should not trouble her further, which was fine with me— fair is fair.

She handed me the piece of paper upon which she had written the books' numbers, and I began to search for them. The *Life of Florence Nightingale* was obviously written for a junior audience and that was fine since for illustrative purposes a work that gets right to the point is just what one needs. *The Complete Alfred Lord Tennyson* was old and worn, and some of the verses were circled, but some of the circled verses seemed to be the most appropriate ones for my sermon.

A History of Christian Missions was not in its place, and I did not bother to search around for it, but when I took the first two books to the desk, she asked, "Were you not able to find the missions book, or did it not suit your need?"

"I was not able to find it," I said, and my voice sounded flat and dull.

Without asking, she took the piece of paper from my hand and said: "Let me give it a try."

She walked from behind the desk, and she moved so smoothly that she seemed to float on air.

"Follow me," she said, smiling at me like an old time movie star.

I followed her to the religion section, and not more than three books over from the place I looked, she found *A History of Christian Missions.*

"This place needs a lot of work," she said, "but I have plenty of time, don't I?"

"Yes, plenty of time around here," I said, "and time to spare."

"What do you do in *your* spare time?" she asked.

I don't have any particular hobbies, and I did not know how to answer.

"Not much," I managed to say. "Sometimes I drive down to Pensacola Beach."

"Well, maybe you could take me along sometime," she said.

You could have pushed me over with a feather. I was not expecting her to make the first move. For that matter, if I had made the first move, I would not have expected her to say yes.

"Yes, yes, good, good," I said, showing way too much excitement.

"Well, when do you want to go, Robert Smith?" she asked.

"Tomorrow evening?" I offered.

"Yes, tomorrow evening would be good for me," she said. "I will see you then. Pick me up at the library at six?"

"Sure," I said.

I took my books and drove from the library straight to the hospital for the day's visitation. I felt good, and it must have been obvious since one of the patients I visited said that my presence had warmed her through and through—something that until then no one had ever said about my presence—and another asked me to pray that he would feel as good as I looked like I felt.

After visitation I drove to the church office. The answering machine light was flashing so I pressed the button and heard Ben Dunning's voice: "Robert, you're not going to believe this, but Langston Long is getting up a petition to close down the library. I could use a quote from you since you are the library's number one patron and a respected member of the community...well, at least you're respected by those who didn't play baseball with you in eleventh grade, but that's another story. Give me a holler."

I picked up the phone, punched in the *Clegmore Progressive's* phone number, and asked for Ben.

"Robert," Ben said, "What are you doing for lunch?"

"Nothing," I said, "Why?"

"Because I'm a little bit swamped right now, but I'll meet you at Grandma's Kitchen at noon."

"So Langston's trying to get the library closed down?" I asked.

"Yup, but I'll have to tell you about it over lunch. I think he's got something else up his sleeve. See you at noon?"

"Noon it is. Bye."

"Bye."

I worked on my Sunday morning sermon and caught up on office work until eleven forty-five. I drove to Grandma's Kitchen, got out of my car, and sat in a rocking chair on the front porch until Ben arrived.

We sat in a booth at the back of the restaurant, as far away from everyone else as possible, and as we waited for our tea, Ben began to tell me about Langston Long's new crusade.

"See, here's the thing, Rob," he said, "Langston has been eyeing the mayor's office for years, and everyone knows it. He's got his following, you know—those old men that sip coffee with him down at The Sweet Shop and their crowd, you know the ones. They're probably the most pessimistic group of human beings on the face of the earth. Langston has been telling them that the library is a big drain on the city's finances and that since we've got libraries at each of the schools, and there's a much bigger library at Newton on the other end of the county, ours is no longer needed. So what does he do?

"He starts a petition to have the library closed, but, Rob, there's no way he'll get enough signatures to pull it off, and he knows it, so I have to ask what his true agenda is, and I think I know. While the petition won't close the library, it will make people believe the library is expensive. When he runs for mayor this fall, one of the main issues will be whether or not the town should allocate funds to upgrade the library, and while the people of this town will not have supported closing the library, they will resist spending *even more* money on it, and they will see electing Langston as a way to keep spending under control. In their minds, electing Langston will balance the issue."

"I think you're right, Ben," I said, "and you should be covering national politics for a big city paper. You've got the instinct, that's for sure."

"Big city, small town—it's all the same, and besides, if I wrote for a big paper, I would only get to write about one subject, and here I get to write about it all. Sports, weddings, traffic accidents—you name it, I write about it. Now, how about a quote? What do you say?"

"Hmmm, how will you title the headline?" I asked.

"How about *Local Minister Outraged?*" Ben asked.

"No way," I said, "I'm not supposed to get outraged. How about *Local Minister Voices Support?*"

"Boring," Ben said, "but if you insist, I guess it'll have to do."

"Good. You got your tape recorder in your pocket?"

"Always," Ben said.

He removed his mini tape recorder from his pocket, placed it on the table, and pressed its record button.

I spoke: "Clegmore is fortunate to have a public library. Wait, scratch that. Clegmore is *blessed* to have a library, and by supporting the library, we are supporting our own well being.

Sure, we have the school libraries, but they're not open after hours and they're not open on Saturdays. Our kids need the public library as much as they need their school libraries, but they're not the only ones who need the library. For many of our senior citizens, a visit to the library is a chance to get out of the house for awhile and spend time in a safe, pleasant environment, and to them, that's no small thing.

"For many of us between childhood and retirement, the library is the only affordable way to read the biggest number of the best books. For many working adults, the library is the only source of information deeper than what is to be found on the internet, but speaking of the internet, for a number of Clegmore's citizens, the library's computers are their only access to it.

"Is that about enough?"

"No, keep going," Ben said.

"I don't sound preachy, do I?"

"Of course you sound preachy, and that's why I called you. You're a preacher, aren't you? A preacher should sound preachy."

"Okay," I said, "Here goes: Take away our ball parks. Let our walking trails grow over. Let potholes form in the pavement, and let the sidewalks crack, but don't let our library go."

"Stop," Ben said, "That's perfect—just what I needed. I knew I could count on you."

"I was just getting wound up," I said.

"Sorry to cut you off then, but speaking of wound up, how would you like to go fishing Saturday morning?"

"I'm afraid I can't," I said.

"Why not? Got a date Friday night?" Ben asked, winking, not suspecting that I actually had one.

"Well, yes, I do."

"Anyone I would know?"

"Not very well, probably," I said.

"Wait a minute. I was right wasn't I? You're taking the new

librarian out, aren't you? Ha! I knew you were interested. I knew it. You work fast too, don't you? I mean she just got here, you sly old dog..."

"No, no, I think it'll be just a friendly date so don't go starting rumors."

"Oh, you can be sure I won't start any rumors. If anyone knew you were dating the local librarian, it would ruin the credibility of your quote for the story."

"I'm not dating... Listen," I said, "I'm just showing her around, and that's all."

"No wonder you got so worked up about the library." Ben said, "A quote like the one you gave is sure to impress her."

"I wasn't thinking about her when...Come on Ben, you know I..."

Ben stared at me with a big, knowing grin, and I couldn't finish my sentence.

After we paid and exited Grandma's Kitchen, Ben popped me on the shoulder with the backside of his right hand and said, "Good luck, old boy. She's a pretty girl. You'll need it."

I drove back to the office, and although I tried to work, in the back of my mind I spent the rest of the afternoon planning my upcoming excursion with the most beautiful woman in the world. I left the office around five, drove back home, changed into some exercise clothes, and headed for the YMCA for a workout. I found that I had lots of excess energy, and I put it to good use, lifting weights, jogging on the treadmill, and playing basketball. By the time I finished, I was pretty tired, but before I could go back home, I had to fill my car's gas tank.

I pulled my car up beside pump number four at Sugg's Stop-n-Save, got out, and started pumping regular into my car's tank. I heard tires squealing, and I turned my head in the direction from which the sound came.

Suddenly I saw Myra Findley's car appear. She must have been going eighty miles per hour. Considering how short a distance she had to reach that speed, it seemed incredible. A second after she passed the gas station, she slammed on her brakes, made a U-turn, drove toward the station, and zoomed over to pump eight.

When she opened her door, she looked exactly like she had looked the previous evening—shoulders slumped, full of nervous energy. I raised my hand to wave at her, but she seemed unaware of her surroundings, and she did not see me or respond in any way. I lowered my hand and watched and listened:

"Gas, gas, gas,
To go fast, fast, fast,
So I won't get passed, passed, passed."

"Myra, how are you?" I asked, raising my voice.

She lowered her head and pretended not to hear.

I shook my head, topped off my tank, and went inside to pay. I wasn't thirsty, but I wanted to speak with her when she came inside so I walked over to the soft drink cooler and searched for a drink. The grape soda and the cream soda looked delicious, but before I could make up my mind, she stepped through the door, laid some money on the counter, apparently the exact amount required, and departed without saying a word. I forgot about the soda and hurried to the door, but by the time I stepped outside, she was cranking her car and leaving. She spun out of the parking lot and vanished in no time flat.

Suddenly a swarm of doubts filled my mind. Did she not recognize me? Had I misunderstood something at the library? Were we really going out the next evening?

When I tried to fall asleep that Thursday night, I found it nearly impossible to do so, and I did not drift off until the wee hours of Friday morning. I kept wondering what would happen on Friday night.

Five

Sunday is a workday for me so I take Fridays off. I spent that Friday morning doing housework, and I had a ham sandwich for lunch. I went for a walk in the early afternoon, and since the air was cold, I felt refreshed when I returned. After I showered and shaved, I put on the clothes I thought were my most attractive and most appropriate for the occasion—a white, button down shirt, a navy blue, v-neck sweater vest, brown corduroy pants, brown socks, and a pair of two tone loafers.

After I dressed, I had a few minutes to kill so I checked my car for the third time that day to make sure it was clean and ready to take out for a date or whatever it was supposed to be. Maybe she was not thinking of it as a date. I went back inside, combed my hair one last time, patted my face with a towel, locked the house, walked back outside, and departed for the library. I didn't want to arrive too early so I drove a lap around town and tried to clear my mind.

At exactly five fifty, I pulled my car into the library parking lot. The library closed at six, and there were only two cars there other than Myra's and my own. I walked inside, and she greeted me with a warm smile and motioned me over to the desk.

"I've got a couple more patrons to check out," she said, "and then we can go."

I stood beside the desk for a minute and watched as a middle-aged woman made her way to it with a stack of novels. Myra stamped her books, and after the woman exited, she placed her elbows on her desk, placed her chin on her elbows, glanced up

39

at an angle, said, "One more to go," and her overall manner made me think of Audrey Hepburn.

A few seconds later, a young man approached the desk with a science fiction novel, and I could tell by the way his eyes lingered when he gazed at Myra that he was quite taken with her beauty. Myra stamped his book, followed him to the door, locked it, and said, "Let me get my coat. I hope the beach won't be too cold. A walk would be nice."

"With your coat on, you'll be warm," I said. "The main problem will be the wind, not the temperature."

For a first date, the hour and a half drive from Clegmore to Pensacola Beach posed the possibility of too much uncomfortable silence, but Myra was a charming conversationalist, and the drive went smoothly. We spoke of our families, the schools we had attended, and Clegmore.

When we were about halfway to the beach, I brought up Langston Long's petition.

"I guess you've heard about the petition, haven't you?" I asked.

She smiled as if my question intrigued her in a positive way. "No, what petition?"

"Oh, you haven't heard? I thought someone would have told you by now."

"Is something wrong?" she asked.

"No. Nothing's wrong, and you don't have anything to worry about."

She raised one eyebrow. "Are you sure?"

"Yes, I'm sure. It's just Langston Long and his gang of complaining buddies—nothing at all to worry about."

"Robert, has someone complained about me already?"

"Not at all, you see... I'd rather not tell you this, but one of the members of Clegmore's city council is getting up a petition to close the library, but it's nothing to worry about since it's only Langston Long and no one outside of his family and his gripe circle can stand him. I know that doesn't sound like something a preacher should say about somebody, but it's true."

"I don't know what to say to this. I've been at the library three days, and already this? Wow. Are you sure?"

"Yes, Myra, I'm sure. I wouldn't make up something like this."

"But you say it's nothing to worry about?"

"I promise you, it's nothing at all, and it's certainly nothing to do with you. Langston's setting himself up for a run for Mayor, that's all. The library's got the local newspaper and most of the folks in Clegmore on its side."

"Then how is this man, what's his name, Mr. Long, setting himself up for a run for Mayor?"

"Ben Dunning, the reporter who introduced us Wednesday, thinks that by circulating the petition, Langston will give people the idea that he'll manage the city's finances rigidly. The petition won't shut the library down, but it'll put the thought in the back of people's minds that it's a big expense. Langston will be viewed as the candidate who will keep the expense under control. The idea makes perfect sense when you think about how people love balance, and besides, Ben's seldom wrong about stuff like that."

"Well, I hope he's not wrong. So far, I rather like Clegmore. Have you lived in Clegmore all your life?"

"Except when I went to college and seminary, yes, I have, and that gives me an idea. I could start a counter-petition for supporters of the library to sign. Clegmore has a Friends of the Library organization to help raise funds. I'm a member, and I could start with the other members."

"Good idea," Myra said. "Langston Long is wrong, wrong, wrong." She covered her mouth with one hand and in a garbled tone talked through her fingers: "Uh, would you stop at a convenience store? I'm sorry. Please?"

"Yes, of course," I said. "Are you okay?"

"I'm okay, but I'm feeling hollow so I'll get some juice to help me swallow." She covered her mouth with her other hand.

I pulled my car into a parking space, and she threw the door open and dashed inside the store. I watched her through the store's plate glass. She chose a bottle of apple juice, carried it to the counter, paid for it, and fumbled through her purse as she rushed into the ladies room. She stayed in the ladies room for a long time, so long that if she had stayed much longer I would have asked the woman at the cash register to go in and check on her, but just before I got overly worried, she emerged looking like royalty on parade.

I watched her as she moved across the convenience store floor and seemed to float an inch off the floor as she walked. I got out, ran around the car, and opened her door. She lowered herself into the passenger seat and crossed her legs like an actress getting into a limo after a movie premiere.

She did not seem nearly as warm or friendly, but whatever she seemed, I liked it, and I was glad to be around it. I felt like a big, big man with a woman like that sitting in the front seat of my car. From the convenience store to Pensacola Beach, we didn't talk much, but I didn't mind. I was too lost in dreams and visions of spending time in the presence of perfect beauty to care.

When we arrived at Pensacola Beach, we thought that since we were both hungry, we should pick a place to eat. We decided on a large seafood restaurant across the street from the water and went inside.

A hostess led us to a table, and a waitress approached our table, gave us menus, and took our drink orders.

"Any recommendations?" Myra asked after the waitress went to get out drinks—a tea for me and a soft drink for Myra.

"The flounder is good," I answered, "but I'm getting the seafood platter—a little bit of everything and so much food I'll take more than half of it home in a to-go box.

"I think I'll have the same," she said. "Would you mind watching my purse while I visit the ladies' room?"

I felt sure she had not actually used the rest room at the convenience store, and I suspected she would do so now. I also suspected that if I opened her purse, which was sitting on the table in front of her seat, I would see one or more pill bottles. I looked at her purse for a few seconds and the temptation to open it made my heart beat fast.

I would do it only to try to understand her better, and there's nothing wrong with that, especially if I could help her, I told myself, but another part of me said, *No, you would be invading her privacy. If she wants you to know about her personal issues, she'll tell you.*

The argument went back and forth inside my mind for a few seconds, and I guessed that the latter voice was the voice of my better judgment, but the voice of curiosity won out. I reached over, unsnapped her purse, and glanced inside. I saw two bottles of prescription drugs. I pushed the purse's flap in place, leaned back in my chair, and tried to look relaxed, but I felt like a creep because of what I had done.

Myra returned from the ladies' room a minute or so later, picked up her purse to place it in one of the empty chairs, and she noticed at the same time I did that its flap was not snapped securely in place.

I'm sure that a look of worry crossed my face as I realized that for fear of pushing her purse off the table, I had failed to push its flap hard enough to make its snap catch. Myra glanced at my face, and she knew what I had done. She didn't say a word about it, but in the way a woman just knows things, she just knew, and she was not pleased. Our eyes met for a second, and I could tell she felt hurt and was slightly angry, but I could also tell that she was not altogether surprised.

A few awkward moments passed, but the silence was broken when the waitress appeared at our table to take our orders. We told her our choices, and I ordered the crab claws appetizer.

As we dipped the crab claws in cocktail sauce and nibbled on the meat, the mood lightened, and Myra restarted the conversation.

"So, what is a minister's life like?" she asked.

"Well, like any other life, I guess, there are some good things about it and some not so good things. The thought that I might be making a difference in some people's lives has to be the best thing, and living under the microscope of public scrutiny has to be the worst. What's a librarian's life like?"

"Probably not like most people think," she said. "I worked in the university library for two years, and I found the work to be diverse and interesting. To be a good librarian, you've got to keep up with information in any number of fields. There are some tedious chores of course, and that's the worst part, but a librarian never stops learning, and that's my favorite part."

Over supper, the conversation was polite, but it did not return to the level it had reached in the car on the way down. My snooping had changed the mood. Still, I sensed that she was not completely put out with me.

After supper, we put our to-go boxes in my car's trunk, drove a short way down the street, and parked beside a long boardwalk. We walked to the place where the sand was compacted at the edge of the water and started to stroll. Silver moonlight danced on the surface of the waves, and the wind blew steadily from the gulf.

"Robert," Myra began at once, "Don't get too interested in me."

"What do you mean?" I asked.

"You know," she said. "Don't think I'm someone you would like to date. I'm not. You have no idea, but if you did, you wouldn't even consider it."

"You really think I wouldn't? Well then, why not?"

"I would rather not talk about why. I know you looked in my purse..."

"Yes, and I am sorry about that," I interrupted. "I was concerned, but I'm very sorry. I shouldn't have looked."

"Concerned and curious, yes, I know. I'm used to it by now. You're not the first, and it doesn't even bother me that much anymore. The thing is, Robert, you're a nice guy. I can tell that, and you don't need to get too entangled with someone like me. I've got some issues. I've had these issues most of my life, and I'm probably not someone you should date, but you will be my friend, won't you?"

"Of course I'll be your friend."

"Good," she said. At the same time, she placed her hand in the crook of my elbow and moved a step closer to me. We strolled that way for half an hour or so, and I felt very confused.

After the stroll, we drove back to Clegmore. I helped her into her car and asked her if she would like me to follow her to her apartment to make sure she got home safely. She said she would like it very much, and I drove behind her and watched her walk inside. She waved goodbye, and I waved back to her and drove to my house as fast as I could.

Ordinarily, I would not call anyone after eleven, but Ben Dunning is a night owl so I took a chance.

Ben answered the phone: "Hello?"

"Hi Ben, this is Rob. I'm not waking you up, am I?"

"Not at all. I was just watching TV. What's up?"

"I've changed my mind about going fishing. You still feel like wetting a hook in the morning?"

"I'd be glad to. Be here at five thirty?"

"That's early, but sure, I'll be there."

"Okay, goodnight then."

Six

Maybe we were talking because the fish were not biting, or maybe the fish were not biting because we were talking, but either way, the only noise on the Alabama River that morning was the sound of our voices.

"She's got issues," Ben said. "So what? What woman, or for that matter, what human being doesn't? Everybody is crazy in some way. Take Terl Joiner, President of the Clegmore Community Bank for instance. You won't find a more intelligent man in Clegmore. He's got a computer for a brain. He reads people like books, and he can negotiate as well as a senator, but if you ever saw him walking down the street having an intense conversation with nobody but himself, both sides of the conversation, out loud, you would think he was a candidate for the loony bin.

"And what about Sandra Wayans the principal's secretary at the elementary school? She's worked her job without a hitch for nearly thirty years. She's a good wife and mother, but there was that one afternoon about twelve years ago when her mind snapped like a half-licked candy cane. A few folks thought it was the stress of the end of the school year. A few others thought it was something that must have been building up inside her for a long time, but most folks didn't think there could be an explanation for why a quiet, middle aged woman would fall down screaming on the floor of old Mr. Jordan's office supply shop, get up, knock over an entire display of calculators, run outside, climb onto the post office's roof, and not come down until the fire department got her mother to coax her.

"So what if she's got issues? If I were you, I wouldn't let it bother me. Doesn't matter what it is—multiple personality, obsessive compulsive, or even schizophrenia—you can work around it."

"Oh come on now. You just think that I'm too old to be picky. What about your wife? She doesn't have issues like that."

"Well, not quite like that. She's got her quirks, but I'm the one who has issues in our family."

"You? No way. I've known you my whole life. What issues?"

"Yes, I do. I don't know what you would call it, but it's the opposite of stress. If I have too much to do, I'm fine, but if I don't have enough to do, I start losing my mind. That's why it's good for me to work at a newspaper—always too much to do—it keeps me sane."

"Speaking of the newspaper, what's the latest on Langston Long's petition?" I asked.

"He's off to a good start. He called in late yesterday afternoon and told me he had eighty five signatures and to be sure to include the figure in the article."

"Are you going to include it?"

"Of course I am. Since he's only been circulating the petition for a couple of days, he thinks that's a large number and an indication of success, and maybe it is, but I'm going to write it like this: 'As of Friday afternoon, fewer than a hundred Clegmore citizens had agreed to sign the controversial petition.' My way makes it sound like the petition is off to a slow start and doomed to fail."

"But Ben, that's not objective reporting."

Ben laughed hard and threw his head back, "Rob, there's no such thing as objective reporting. It's better to report something with an honest slant than to slant it and lie about it the way the big papers do. I'll also write an editorial on the subject so no one will misunderstand my position, you know, for honesty's sake."

"I told Myra about the petition."

"Oh yeah? How did she take it?"

"Not well, but then she had other things on her mind, her issues, you know."

"I hope you told her she had nothing to worry about," Ben said.

"I did, and I went a step further than that. I told her I would start a petition for supporters of the library."

"Way to go!" Ben said. "You're going to give me some good headlines yet. Wait just a minute, will ya?"

Ben reached into his tackle box and removed a wireless phone. He extended its antenna, pressed its buttons, and waited.

"This won't take long," he said. "I'm calling our graphics and design guy."

We sat in silence for a moment then he said: "Hello. This is Ben. Have you laid out the article about the library yet? No? Good. I need you to add something to it: 'Rev. Robert Smith is starting his own petition for those who support the Clegmore Public Library. Clegmoreans who strongly support the library should stop at the office of the Progressive or at the library itself to obtain and distribute copies of the petition for the collection of signatures.' Have you got that? Good. Lay it in right after the part about Langston's obtaining less than a hundred signatures. Thanks. Bye."

"Thanks," I said. "You really do work fast, don't you?"

"Yep, and after she reads this article, you'll have no trouble reeling in Myra Findley."

"Speaking of reeling," I said, "The fish aren't biting. You want to try another spot?"

"Sure," Ben said as he cranked his boat's motor and steered us downstream.

We fished until noon, but we did not catch anything. We would have stayed longer, but rain clouds were forming, and we thought we should get off the river. We ate at the landing,

49

loaded Ben's boat, and drove back to Clegmore. Ben dropped me off at my house, and feeling sleepier than I had felt in as long as I could remember, I went inside, and stretched out on the sofa for a long afternoon nap. Not long after I lay down, it started raining, and that made my sleep deep and peaceful.

A couple hours later someone knocked on my door, and I forced my eyes open.

Seven

I opened the door, and my sleepiness vanished when I saw who was standing under a red umbrella.

"How did you know where I lived?" I asked.

"Aren't you going to invite me in from this rain?" Myra asked.

"Oh, uh, yeah, sure. Sorry. I didn't mean to be rude. Please do come in."

"I asked one of the library patrons this morning. Everybody knows everybody else in this town, don't they?" she said as she closed her umbrella and came inside.

"Almost everybody," I said. "Can I help you in some way?"

"It's Saturday night, and other than my cat, I have no one to keep me company. You want to do something for fun?"

"Like what?" I asked.

"Well, we could rent a couple of movies and take them back to my apartment. I got a DVD player for Christmas. Like most of my stuff, it's still boxed up, but you could get it out and hook it up to my TV, couldn't you?"

"Yeah, and that sounds fun, but I'm a preacher, and you're the town librarian, and if anyone sees my car parked in front of your apartment for any length of time after dark, people will talk."

"So what if they do?" she asked. "But if it bothers you, I'll drive us over in my car and drive you back when the movie is over. No one will ever know you were there."

"Well, why not?" I said. "Give me a minute to get ready."

I hurried into my bedroom and put on jeans and a sweatshirt. I grabbed my coat on the way out the door, and we got into her car.

As she pulled out of my driveway, she accelerated so smoothly that I could tell the car was moving only because the scenery was passing, and she turned each corner with precision, signaling at just the right times, and coming to complete stops at stop signs but lingering no longer than necessary.

When we arrived at the video rental store, I asked her what kind of movies she liked best, and she said she preferred romantic comedies but was open to watching just about anything that didn't have too much violence or crude language. As we searched the shelves, I was glad to see that except for a few of my favorite action flicks, she liked the same movies I liked.

We picked *Bringing Up Baby,* which I had never seen, and *Forrest Gump,* which she had never seen. She drove us back to her apartment, and after we went inside, she found the box that held her DVD player. I got it out and started trying to figure out which wires connected to which receptacles. As I worked, she went to a room in the rear of her apartment to change into some casual clothes, and her cat, a big calico with mismatched eyes, approached me and rubbed against my leg.

"What's your cat's name?" I raised my voice to ask.

"GB," she answered.

"Is it a male or a female?"

"Male," she said.

"Why did you name him GB?"

"You can't guess?" she asked when she returned to the room.

"Should I be able to?"

"Yeah, just look at him."

"Oh," I said. "He has one green eye and one blue eye—GB."

"You guessed it."

"I think I've got this thing connected. Which movie do you want to watch first?"

"Let's start with *Bringing Up Baby.* It's mostly just light hearted comedy."

I started the movie, she turned off the lights, and we sat on her couch. We both started giggling early on, and several times during moments of intense laughter, she touched my arm. I liked the fact that she felt comfortable enough to touch me, but I felt awkward about it too. Even if she was the most beautiful woman in the world at times, I didn't know where things were going with her.

After we finished watching *Bringing Up Baby*, we ordered a pizza, and as we waited for it to arrive, we started watching *Forrest Gump*. As we sat in the darkness, thoughts of her other side kept running through my mind, and I realized that even though she was remarkably beautiful, Myra Findley must have been a very lonely woman. Of course anyone would be lonely after four days in a new town, but surely her loneliness ran much deeper.

When the pizza deliverer knocked on the door, I pressed the pause button on the DVD player, and she turned on the light and opened the door.

"Here," I said as I removed my wallet and took out a twenty dollar bill, "this should cover it."

She handed the twenty to the pizza deliverer, and when he offered her change, I told him to keep the difference.

"Is that Brother Rob?" he asked.

"Yes, it's me," I said, and I stepped to her door to see who had recognized me by my voice.

The pizza deliverer was Wade Garner, a senior at Clegmore High School and a member of my church's youth group. His mother attended my church and so did her mother.

"Keep the change," I told him.

Wade said goodbye, and Myra closed the door.

"By tomorrow, half the town will be talking about us," I said.

"Why should that bother you?" she asked. "I don't get it."

"I'll try to explain it after we eat."

She gave me a polite but puzzled smile and nodded agreement. Warmth flowed from her every feature, and I reminded myself of Ben's advice. Everyone has at least some small problem, and surely I had exaggerated the extent of her problem. I told myself that it was no big deal that occasionally she got a little nervous and rhymed her sentences. At that moment, I felt like the luckiest man in the world because I was sharing a pizza with the most beautiful woman in the world.

Our pizza, which we had ordered with double cheese, sausage, and pepperoni, was delicious, and its aroma was intoxicating. When we were both full, she turned the lights back off, and I restarted the movie.

A few minutes later, she leaned against me and whispered: "So, why don't you want anyone to know about our seeing one another? What's the big deal?"

"I don't know," I said. "It's just that I'd rather keep my private life private, I guess. And also, I guess, I'll lose credibility with my petition if people think I have an ulterior motive. We wouldn't want people to think I was circulating it just to try to impress you."

"I suppose we wouldn't," she said. "People are nosy so we can't get cozy."

She covered her mouth.

"I'd better drive you home now," she said.

"But we haven't finished the movie."

"You've seen it before," she said, "and I'll finish it tomorrow so feel no sorrow."

She covered her mouth again.

"It's fine," I said. "I understand."

"No you don't, and I'm not lying, but thanks for trying. We'd better go. Come now. Don't be slow."

We walked outside, and I noticed immediately that the rain had stopped. She raced ahead of me, unlocked the passenger door, and walked around the back of her car to the driver's side. When she was directly behind the car, she paused for a second, reached down, grabbed a handful of mud and slung it on her

54

tag. This seemed an odd thing to me, and I should have given it more thought at the time, but I was trying so hard to figure out the rest of her behavior that I barely paused to consider it.

She had the engine cranked before I had time to sit down, and as soon as I closed my door, she slammed the gearshift into reverse, stomped the gas pedal, and jerked the car out of its parking space. I felt my entire body lurch forward, and I reached for my seatbelt, pulled it across my stomach, and struggled to fasten it.

At the exit from her apartment complex, she floored the accelerator, squealed her tires, and sprayed road gravel in the air.

"The cops are pretty tough about speed limits in this part of town so..." I began to say, intending to finish the sentence with, "you might want to take it easy," but before I could get all the words out of my mouth she countered: "I'm in a hurry, but don't you worry, and don't tell me how to drive. I'll get you home alive."

"Okay," I said as I tried to make myself comfortable.

She screeched to a halt on McKay and Eighth, and I had to brace myself with one hand against her dash to keep from being thrown into the windshield. I glanced at her out of the corner of my eye, and she wore a sadistic smile on her face. She hit the accelerator again, and the car heaved forward.

Upon a sudden reflexive urge, I reached toward the steering wheel, but before my hand touched it, she swatted it away. She looked straight at me, and the expression on her face said: "Try that again, and I'll bite your hand off."

At that moment, blue, flashing lights came on, and we both turned and saw a police car pull in behind us.

"If I let him get close, he'll surely catch us, but if I stomp it now, he'll never match us," she said.

"Are you crazy? Myra, just pull over, and everything will be fine."

"How dare you say such a thing to me? I'll have you know

I'm as sane as can be!"

"I didn't mean it like that. Listen, just slow down, please."

She turned and grinned at me, and I knew that further pleading would be useless. I felt the latch on my seatbelt to make sure it was fastened securely, braced my feet against the front side of the floorboard, held on to the handgrip above my head, and prayed.

The officer chased us, and I realized that she had thrown mud on her tag for precisely this reason. If the police tried to pull her over for speeding, an extremely common thing in small towns, and she made a successful getaway, they would not be able to identify the car.

The police car pulled to within inches of touching her back bumper, and I could hear its siren's deafening scream and see its blue lights flashing like lightning.

At a four way intersection, she made a hard ninety degree turn, and for a second she lost the officer, but another officer pulled in from a side street about half a mile up the road, and I felt sure we would be sandwiched between the police cars.

She slammed on her brakes again, turned a hundred and eighty degrees and drove back to the intersection where the first officer was just getting his car turned in the right direction.

Although I thought her behavior was insane, I had to admit it was a brilliant tactic. For several seconds, we were completely in the clear in a neighborhood with many cut across streets and no dead ends.

I thought we had escaped, but ahead of us a third car appeared, and I lost confidence.

"Myra, why are you doing this?" I asked, but she did not answer.

She turned down a small lane, turned onto another, turned again, backed into a driveway and flipped her lights off.

We sat in perfect silence for several seconds until we saw the blue lights and heard the screaming sirens pass one street over from where we were parked.

The moment the cars passed, she flipped on her lights, pulled back into the street, and drove in the direction of my house. When we reached my driveway, she pulled in and said: "See ya."

I got out of her car as fast as I could, closed its door, and watched as she pulled onto Eighth Avenue and took off like a rock from a slingshot. For a few minutes all I could do was stand on the lawn, shake my head, and scratch my chin.

I felt many things, but mostly I just felt confused because strangely enough, I was still interested in her, and I couldn't deny it.

Eight

I went to the church office early Sunday morning and used the church's computer to write the petition to counter Langston Long's petition. I ran off thirty copies of the petition on the church's copier, and since it was not official church business, I had to leave three dollars, a dime for each copy, in the small cardboard box in the copier room as copier rules required.

I never mention political issues—even local, seemingly benign issues like library support—during church services, but that Sunday I broke my rule and mentioned my petition during the time in the service after the sermon designated for announcements.

"I'm sure you've all heard by now that there's a petition going around to close the Clegmore Public Library. Well, I'm starting a petition for anyone who wishes to express support for our library," I said, "and I wouldn't bring it up in church were it not for the fact that it directly affects my ministry. As most of you know, I lean pretty heavily on the library for help with researching my sermons. I've placed copies of the petition in the church foyer, and anyone wishing to sign it may do so after the close of the service."

The great majority of Shiloh Baptist Church's members signed my petition so the line out the church's main door moved slower than usual, and this provided Linda Delchamp time to start a conversation with me: "I hear you and the new librarian have taken a shine for each other."

"Where on earth did you hear a thing like that?" I asked.

"My cousin Renee Garner's sister-in-law is Lucy Garner, Wade Garner's mother. Wade is a pizza deliverer, and Renee called me last night, and..."

"Okay, okay, enough already. Yes, I have spent some time with Miss Findley, but I'm just getting to know her, really. For now we're only friends, and for all I know, we may never be more than that."

"Ha! You should hope you WILL be more than that. Friday I stopped at the library on my lunch break. She's a pretty girl, and you're not getting any younger."

"Oh gee, thanks," I said.

"I'm just kidding with you, but seriously, she seems very nice. Don't let a good thing pass you by."

She had to move up in the line so we weren't able to continue the conversation, but before she reached the door, she said: "By the way, the mayor and most of the city council are siding with you on this library matter. I wouldn't take Langston Long too seriously."

After everyone had filed out, I collected the petitions, turned off the lights, and locked up. I drove from the church to Sugg's Stop-n-Save and bought a copy of the *Progressive*.

Kyleen Tanner, the pleasant bleached blonde working the register, said: "Hey, you're on the front page this week. You're having it out with Langston, huh?"

"Nah. I'm just fighting to save the library. You want to sign my petition?"

"I wish I could, but Langston's brother owns this place."

"I understand," I said.

Just then it occurred to me for the first time that saving the library might be at least somewhat difficult. After all, Langston came from a large family that had many connections in Clegmore. He had brothers, sisters, nieces, nephews, and cousins working at the banks, the shops, the post office, the city hall, the public works, the police force, the hospital, the YMCA, the chamber of commerce, and everywhere else. You name it, Langston had a connection to it, and in Clegmore politics "connection" is the word above all words.

Most of our restaurants close on Sundays, but the catfish place nine miles north of town beside the interstate stays open so I drove there for lunch. I ordered the catfish filet basket and read the paper while I waited for the basket to arrive. Ben had written the article in such a way that it seemed that Langston Long and I had a direct debate and an intense one at that. I wasn't sure how to feel about that, but I couldn't help feeling happy that he had given me the last word and had slanted most of the article to the pro-library side of the issue.

A photo of Langston appeared on the left side of the page, and a photo of me appeared on the right. I do not know when Ben snapped my picture, but he caught me talking, and to supplement an argument, this seemed most appropriate.

My meal came, and as I ate, three people approached my table. The first two expressed complete agreement with my position, but the third, a scrawny, rat-faced man who drank coffee with Langston most mornings, said that he hoped I didn't take his signing Langston's petition personally and that he wished everyone could get along.

"Let me ask you something," I asked him. "Did you sign his petition because you genuinely think the library should be closed, or did you do it because of peer pressure?"

"I just wish everyone could get along," he mumbled and walked away, scratching his head.

I had finished lunch and was about to stand and leave when Langston Long himself entered the restaurant. He was wearing a red sport coat, which made his big red face seem even redder. When he saw me, he walked straight to my table. I didn't know what he intended to say, and I feared the worst, but just before he reached me, he put on his best salesman smile and extended his right hand for a shake.

"I have seen the enemy," he said with an overly friendly laugh, "and you're him. No, just kidding there, Reverend Smith. I enjoyed reading your comments in the paper this morning. The *Progressive* made it sound like we squared off, didn't it?"

"It sure did," I said as I tried to laugh with him.

"Well, this should be fun, don't you think? There's nothing like a good public debate."

"Yes, public debate is good," I said, "but I can't imagine this being very fun for the new librarian."

"And you would be concerned about the new librarian, wouldn't you?" he continued without losing his smile.

"What do you mean?"

"I think you know what I mean. My nephew, Warren Long, works for the Clegmore PD, and last night there was some funny business over on Eighth Avenue. It involved a car matching the description of one they found parked at the McKay apartment complex later that night."

"The policeman didn't get its tag number?" I asked.

"Apparently the car made a U-turn before the officer's dash camera got a clear shot, but the incident is being studied. They're sending the videotape to a lab in Montgomery. Of course they know who the car at the McKay complex belongs to, but they can't imagine that a woman in her respected profession would take a police cruiser on a high speed chase."

"There was no high speed chase," I blurted out and realized immediately that I had put my foot in my mouth.

"Why, Reverend Smith, how would you know there was no high speed chase?"

"Uh well, I live on Eighth, and I didn't hear anything last night," I said.

"My nephew says there was a passenger in the car. He says the video is so dark you can barely make out the passenger's silhouette, but there definitely was a passenger."

I looked at my watch and said: "Sorry, Langston, I've got to run. Maybe we can talk some other time. No hard feelings on the library debate, huh?"

"Reverend Smith, you insult me. Of course there are no hard feelings. This is nothing personal, nothing personal at all—just good public discourse."

"Good, let's keep it that way, please," I said, attempting to return his smile.

We shook hands again, and I paid and left the restaurant. On the way home I kept replaying the things that Langston said. I had been seen in Myra's apartment, no getting around it. Myra had run from a police officer, and the film of her escape would most likely be analyzed at state headquarters, and there was a good chance their experts could somehow identify the car, especially since Myra was already a suspect. I did not like the way it all made me feel.

The thing I like to do most on a Sunday afternoon is take a nap, and I was fully intending to take one when I got home, but the moment I walked through the door, I saw that I had a message on my answering machine. I pressed the play button, and I heard Myra's voice:

"Rob, we need to talk. A couple of police officers came by this morning asking me some questions. My number is 3456. Please call as soon as you get this. Bye."

I picked up the phone and pressed in the first three digits, which are the same for everyone in Clegmore, followed by the last four, which she had given.

"Hello?" she said.

"It's me, Rob."

"Good, we've got to talk. Can you come over?"

"Yeah, sure. I'll be there in a few minutes."

Myra opened her apartment door the moment I got out of my car. She stood in the doorway, and framed thus, she looked like the masterpiece of some famous Renaissance artist.

"Are you okay?" I asked, but she did not answer until I was

inside and the door was closed behind me.

"I'm okay for now," she said, "but I need to ask you a very serious question. Did I do anything, you know, strange last night?"

"How do you define 'strange'?" I asked.

"Sometimes I get a little bit, you know, hyperactive," she said. "Anyway, just tell me if I did anything that could get me in trouble with the police."

"You don't remember?"

"I don't. That's the other side of it, and I hope you won't think less of me for it, but sometimes I don't recall some things that I do."

"You really don't remember?" I asked.

"I don't."

"A cop tried to pull you over, and you lost him."

"No, you're kidding! Did I really do that?"

"Yes, you really did."

"Wow!"

"Exactly."

"I don't think I've ever done that before," she said.

She stood speechless for several awkward moments before she continued: "Rob, I don't like to talk about this, but you know already that I have to take medicine."

"Yeah, I know," I said, "and I'm sorry about that."

"It's okay," she said. "You shouldn't have looked in my purse, but at least you were concerned—not that that excuses you. About my medicine—I had it pretty well regulated before I moved here, but I think the new working and living environment has upset my balance. My highs seem too high, and I guess my lows seem too low, but I don't fully remember my lows, and that's the worst thing. Anyway, what I'm getting at, and I truly hate to impose, and I wouldn't ask you to do this if the circumstances weren't extreme, but the thing is, I need someone to look out for me for the next couple of days until I can get my doses regulated."

I glanced into her eyes and without a moment's hesitation said: "Yes, of course."

Nine

She got her purse, and I drove her to my house.

After I parked I asked: "Is there anything in particular that I am supposed to be watching for?"

"I'm not sure," she said, "but if I start acting strange, just be sure to make me take my medicine."

We walked inside, and she sat in my recliner, removed a magazine from the holder to her left, and started scanning it.

I lay down on the couch, kicked off my dress shoes, used the remote control to turn on the TV, and started going through the channels. I stopped at each channel and asked her if the program interested her until we both agreed on one—a PBS show about the history of submarines.

Although the documentary was interesting enough, I fell asleep, and I must have slept soundly because when I woke up, I felt completely refreshed.

I looked at the TV. It was set on one of the shopping networks. I turned around and glanced in the direction of my recliner and sat up straight when I saw that Myra was not there.

"Oh no," I mumbled under my breath as I stood. I called out: "Myra?"

She did not answer. I suddenly felt fear and shame—fear because I did not know exactly what I was supposed to have been watching for, and it could have been something much worse than what I had already seen, and shame because I had failed her.

I ran outside wearing my socks, and though the ground was

cold, I made a full lap around the house and called her name several times. Thinking that I should search the whole neighborhood and alert others to search too, I ran back inside intending to put my sneakers on, but when I entered my bedroom, there she was, lying on top of the covers, sound asleep.

When I stepped inside the room, she opened her eyes and smiled.

"I hope you don't mind me lying here, but there was nowhere else for me to take a nap, and it wasn't fair that you got to sleep and I didn't," she said with a yawn and a smile.

"No problem, I guess," I said, "but I was worried. I thought you might have... you know... you might have..."

"I might have hurt myself?"

"Right, yes, you might have hurt yourself."

"No, and I feel fine. Maybe I'm starting to adjust. Still, I wouldn't want to be left alone."

"That reminds me: Church starts at seven on Sunday evenings, and I have to be there at six thirty to open up. That gives us another hour before we have to leave. You want a snack or something?"

"You didn't say anything about going to church," she said.

"Oh, that's right. You said you don't go to church. Do you practice a different religion?"

"No." she said.

"Are you an atheist, then?" I asked.

"No, I believe in God, same as you. It's not God I have a problem with. It's church itself. When I was a kid, I had a bad experience at a church, but I'd rather not talk about it."

"I understand," I said. "You don't have to come along if you don't want, but I definitely have to go and preach. Will you be okay staying here by yourself for about an hour and a half?"

"Honestly, I'd rather not be alone," she said. "I guess I will go, but you'll need to take me by my apartment so I can change into some church clothes."

"At our church, you don't have to dress up, especially on a Sunday evening. What you're wearing looks fine."

"Are you sure? I mean, I'm wearing jeans and a sweatshirt."

"Of course I'm sure. You're wearing the same kind of clothes that most of our ladies wear. Sunday evening is all about casual."

"I don't remember church being like that."

"Maybe the church you attended wasn't like that. Our church hasn't always been the way it is. At some point, though, we realized that Jesus was a common man, a man of the people, not a Pharisee, and we decided that we should be common too."

"Well, okay. I'll give it a try, but please don't ask me to say or do anything, and I would like to sit in the back."

"You may sit wherever you like," I told her.

After she decided to go to church, she took her purse into my bathroom to redo her make-up and restyle her hair, and while I sat on the couch waiting for her, I pondered the fact that when she seemed weak, I felt strong, but when she seemed strong, I felt weak. I asked myself why my feelings ran to such extremes, and it occurred to me that I had some kind of insecurity. I felt a deep sense of inadequacy about my level of attractiveness to the opposite sex and only when a woman was at her worst did I feel her equal. When a woman was at her best, I felt inferior to her.

Though this was an unpleasant revelation to me, I was glad I experienced it. I had no idea what had caused me to have this insecurity, but at least I knew what my problem was, and that, I thought, could be the first step toward eliminating it.

As I sat thinking, she returned to the living room looking more beautiful than ever. I looked up as she walked through the door, and my mouth fell open. She smiled her prettiest smile, and I felt nervousness rise in my stomach.

With pure grace, she moved across the room, sat in the recliner, and said: "How much longer before we leave?"

"Anytime now," I said. "Are you ready?"

"Yes. Are you?"

She was back to her most intimidating form. I felt no intimidation when she was at her worst and only a little intimidation when she was in between, which she had been for most of the afternoon, but just then I felt the full force of her feminine charm, and I was blown away.

"Let's go then," I managed to say.

We arrived at the church before anyone else, and as I went about turning on lights and adjusting thermostats, I gave her a quick tour of the facilities. The tour ended at my office, and there she looked through my personal collection of books.

"I see you're a fan of C.S. Lewis," she said.

"Yes—always have been. His Narnia books were my favorites when I was a kid, and since I've grown up, I've read most of his theology. Are you a fan of his?"

"I've never read any of his books, but I know his work has a big following. Maybe I should try one. Any suggestions?"

"Yes. Start with *Mere Christianity*. Here, take my copy. Return it at your convenience." I said.

"Now there's a twist, a librarian returning a book to a library patron."

We chuckled and left my office, and when we reached the church sanctuary, she hurried to the back pew and took a seat. Church members began to arrive, and I greeted each one at the door. They in turn greeted Myra, and she returned their friendliness.

At seven, the service began with singing. Myra opened a hymn book, but she did not sing along with the rest of the congregation.

When the time for the sermon came, I felt a strange mixture of emotion. On the one hand, I was about to do the one thing I felt most comfortable doing—addressing a crowd—but on the other hand, a beautiful woman at her intimidating best was in the crowd, and by default I would be speaking to her too.

I did not know how I should feel, but I decided it would be

best if I tried to forget she was there and speak in my usual manner. This I did, and I must have succeeded because after the service when we were driving to her house, Myra said: "Wow, you really come alive when you preach, don't you?"

"So I'm told," I said. "What did you think of the sermon?"

"Well, I didn't think I would be saying this, but I enjoyed it. You made some very interesting points about the personal benefits of following Christ's ethical teachings—I have never heard the Bible taught that way. I thought we were supposed to be good or else."

"Or else what?" I asked.

"You know. We're supposed to be good or else something very bad will happen to us when we die."

Her personality was swinging away from the apex of feminine perfection toward her other side, and while she was near the center of her cycle, I felt most comfortable talking with her.

"If a person were being good merely to avoid punishment, would that constitute real spiritual goodness or would that constitute the fulfilling of an obligation?"

"The fulfilling of an obligation," she said. "Isn't that what the Bible is all about? Thou shalt do this, or thou shalt not do that?"

"No, it's not about that. We fulfill God's commandments when we have love in our hearts, love of God and love for our neighbor. If we behave out of obligation, we remain selfish to the core."

"That's a good way to look at it," she said. "I know I've always felt better doing things because I loved to do them instead of doing them because I had to. Did you come up with that yourself?"

"No. Jesus did."

"He said that? I never heard that Jesus said that."

"What kind of church did you attend when you were growing up?"

"I don't think it was affiliated with any particular denomination," she said. "The things they said at this church scared me pretty badly."

"That's why you stopped going?" I asked.

"Oh no. Something else happened, but I told you I don't want to talk about it."

"You don't have to," I said.

When we reached her apartment, I walked her inside, and she asked if I would stay and watch her until she fell asleep.

"I can feel myself getting off balance, but if I can fall asleep soon," she said, "I'm certain I won't have any trouble for the rest of the night."

"Sure, no problem." I said.

"How much time can you spend at the library tomorrow?" she asked.

"Except for my routine stops, which only take a couple of hours, I can spend the whole day."

"Good. Will you pick me up for work?"

"Yes. I'd be happy to pick you up."

"Goodnight, then."

"Goodnight," I said.

I sat in a chair beside her bed until her breathing became slow and regular, then I exited her apartment quietly, being careful not to wake her up. On my way home I reflected on how utterly strange it all was. Five days ago, I had been living out my ordinary bachelor life, not expecting anything unusual, especially the appearance and seeming interest of a beautiful woman, and here I was confused and conflicted about whether I had experienced love at first sight or was falling in love or was not falling in love at all.

Ten

I parked in front of Myra's apartment the next morning and went to knock on her door, but she came out before I reached it. When I opened my car's passenger door for her, I asked her how she was doing, and she answered: "Honestly, Rob, not bad but not very well either. Maybe I'll feel better once I'm in the library. My work forces me to concentrate, and when I concentrate I feel better."

"Listen," I said, "I don't presume to know about... You know... I don't assume..."

"Just say it," she said. "And don't worry about hurting my feelings."

"Well, a psychiatrist from Montgomery, Dr. Hernandez, visits the Clegmore Community Hospital each Wednesday. Several people who have come to me for counseling have had conditions that seemed to require medical attention, and I have referred them to him. So far, I haven't heard any complaints, and most of those I've referred have gotten better. Also, I've spoken to him, and he's a nice guy. I don't know. I was thinking maybe you'd like to make an appointment. If you're not comfortable, I could make one for you if you like, or whatever you think."

"I told you not to worry about hurting my feelings," she said. "I had been thinking that an appointment with a doctor is just what I need, and I'm glad you mentioned that one visits the local hospital because I was afraid I was going to have to ask you to drive me to one in a larger city."

"By the way, I brought some petitions to place in the library."

"Oh good!"

When we arrived at the library, she picked up the Sunday and Monday edition of the *Pensacola News Journal*. She unlocked the door, and I held it open for her.

She walked inside, and I tried to inject a little humor: "Feel better already?"

"Believe it or not, yes, I do feel better. There's something about libraries that calms my mind. When I was small, the library was my favorite place to visit. I could get lost in the books and be happy for hours."

After she went to her office, I placed a copy of the petition on the main desk, took a recent issue of the *National Review* from the magazine rack, sat in the most comfortable chair, and started reading.

A few minutes later, the day's first patron arrived, a tall man who looked like he hadn't had much sleep. He placed the third installment of the *Left Behind* series in the return slot and went to find the fourth. When he reached the desk, Myra exited her office, stamped the book's cards, and sent him on his way.

"Wait," I said before he walked away. He stopped, and I stood and approached him. "I've started a petition for people who would like to express support for the library's continued existence in Clegmore. Could I interest you in signing it?"

"Yes," he said, "but it's got to be fast 'cause I'm in a hurry."

I showed him the petition. He signed it with haste, and nearly tripped over me as he turned and darted away.

"The plot must have him hooked," I said out loud.

Myra smiled and placed her right index finger over her lips: "Shhhhh."

"Sorry, forgot where I was for a second."

The second and third patrons appeared to be secretaries on their way to work. They returned books but did not check out additional books, and with enthusiasm, they both signed the petition. When things started to pick up and it was clear that Myra was off to a good day, I told her I needed to spend some time at the church office and asked if she would be okay without me.

She said she felt confident she would be okay, but she hoped that I would check back around noon. I told her I would be happy to and asked what she was doing for lunch.

"My assistants don't arrive until three so I'll be eating a late lunch. I'll send one of them to get me a sandwich from that shop up the street."

"Hey, I could get you something before then," I said.

"You picked up on my hint," she said. "Good, a man with perception. I like that."

"What would you like?" I asked.

"I'd like a turkey on white, light on the mayo, heavy on the mustard."

"Alright, see you at noon."

Myra had been close to her emotional center for the entire morning, and I had been able to talk to her with ease, but at noon when I returned from the church office, it was apparent she had taken her medicine because she was in her top form. Abnormal amounts of beauty and grace radiated from her being, and I could barely speak in her presence.

"Lunch," I said, half choking back the words.

"Thank you," she said with a lilt in her voice ordinarily reserved for queens thanking knights for saving kingdoms.

She ate her sandwich while standing behind the circulation desk, and the motion of her jaw was so graceful that if I had not seen her take a bite from time to time, I would not have known that she was chewing food. I had a roast beef on toast, and I'm pretty sure that anyone watching me would have recognized that I was chomping a sandwich.

After lunch, I hung around the library and searched for material for my sermon series on the subject of Priorities. Occasionally I would glance at Myra and she would wink at me.

All seemed well with her, and I could not help thinking that perhaps she had adjusted and that she could keep her mind from reaching its troubled state.

After an hour had passed, I felt confident that she would be fine without me, and I asked: "Would you mind if I go and take care of some business and come back at closing time?"

"I suppose not," she said. "The library closes at six. See you then."

After I made my usual rounds at the hospital, I called Clegmore's only radio station, AM 1040, and asked the DJ to announce that I was circulating a petition, and anyone wishing to sign it could do so at the library. He said he would add the information to the community bulletin board program that aired three times a day, and I thanked him.

I took copies of the petition, drove to the center of town and went for a walk. I stopped pedestrians and entered most of the businesses.

The guys who ran the American Karate Center had just arrived, and were getting ready to teach their after-school classes, and not only did they agree to sign the petition, one of them went next door to Blount's Copiers and Computers and ran off copies to offer the karate students.

Nina Batson and Elizabeth Compton, the ladies who run Beth's Bridal Boutique, both signed because they both used the library on a regular basis.

Ken McDaniel of Ken's Bow and Blade politely but firmly refused to sign because, as he put it: "Ain't many people use the library no more, and taxes is too high in this town, and it needs to go."

Jack Jarvis at Jarvis Appliance said he basically agreed with my side, but he did not want to get involved because as the owner of small business he could not afford to alienate anyone. I'm sure he told those on the other side the same thing.

All but one of the employees at Clegmore Hardware signed,

and Keith Phillips, a long time floor assistant said with much emotion, "My wife and I both work, but it's hard to make ends meet sometimes, and if it wasn't for the library, our kids wouldn't have much opportunity to read. I appreciate your good work. Keep it up."

Lashanda Jackson at Lashanda's Ladies' Luxuries, a store on the north side of town that stocks colorful African dresses, said she would be happy to sign it and asked for additional copies to pass along to her customers and friends.

My efforts were going smoothly until I entered Polk's Pawn Shop and asked Ward Polk, a short bald man, if he would like to sign my petition, and he said: "There's no way on earth I'd sign that worthless piece of paper. My cousin knows what's best for this town, and he's trying to do what's right, and you should be ashamed of yourself for going against him."

"I had forgotten. You and Langston are cousins on his mother's and your father's side, right?"

"Yup, and I'm proud of it, and I don't take too kindly to a hot-shot do-gooder like yourself trying to tear him down. What makes you think you know so much?"

"I don't think I know much, and that's why I want to keep the library alive," I said "so I can learn."

I thought I had made a clever reply and that it would lighten the mood, but Ward turned red in the face. He tried to reply, but he was so mad he could only make gurgling sounds and spit.

"I'd better get going," I said as I pushed open the door and exited his shop.

As the door swung shut, I heard him bark: "That's right, you'd better get going, you up-start hot-shot do-gooder know-it-all."

After I left Polk's, I made a few more stops, collected a few more signatures, and drove to the library. I arrived about thirty minutes before closing time, randomly grabbed a book from the biography section, *Joe DiMaggio: the Hero's Life*, and sat at one of the research tables while Myra finished her duties.

She helped a third grader find a book for a book report, and when she addressed the little girl directly, the child's face seemed to glow with wonder and pride, and I could tell right away that Myra had that unusual charm that some people have with children, an appeal that comes only from gentleness and sincerity.

At six, she closed the library for the day, and we drove to her apartment.

"So, how many people signed the petitions on the circulation desk?" I asked as I accelerated out of the library parking lot.

"Thirty-seven," she said. "I kept track all day."

"I got forty-eight more in town," I said. "A few of my church members are circulating it too, and I hope we're ahead of Langston by now. The midweek edition of the *Progressive* comes out Wednesday afternoon, and I'll need to give Ben a tally by Tuesday night."

When we reached her apartment, Myra said: "Rob, you don't have to stay if you don't want. For one who barely knows me, you've been a good friend to me the last couple of days. Besides, I feel tired, and I think I'll be heading off to sleep soon."

Without giving much thought to the intent of her words, I told her not to hesitate to call if she needed me, said good evening, and departed, but as I drove, her words sank in, and I began to question each one.

By telling me I did not have to stay did she really mean that she did not wish for me to stay? By telling me I had been a good friend to her did she mean she thought of me only as someone to befriend and would never think of me as a man to date? I had always been a "nice guy," and as such I had won much friend-ship but little romantic interest from females.

I thought hard about the subject: Had my niceness been per-ceived as weakness? Or worse, was I really just weak and using "niceness" as a cover? If indeed I was weak, was my weakness connected to or perhaps one and the same with the feelings of inferiority that I had recognized in myself on the previous afternoon?

Myra had made an appointment with the psychiatrist on Wednesday. Maybe I needed to make one too.

Eleven

Until Myra got off work, Tuesday was something of a repeat of Monday. I collected more signatures and retrieved some of the petitions I had given to others to circulate. From the library, I called the numbers in to Ben and asked him how we were doing. He said that Langston had just called in his numbers, and he was ahead by sixty-one. He told me not to worry about it though since Langston had a head start and I had some good people on my side.

After Ben and I hung up, Myra locked up, and I started to drive her to her apartment, but she said she felt like getting a burger and offered to treat if I wanted one too.

"Sure, and I know just the place," I said.

We got onto Highway Thirty-one and drove three miles beyond the city limits to Sunny's Super Cream.

Sunny's has a giant, plastic statue of an ice cream cone in front. Year round the cone is covered with orange Christmas lights, and the ice cream is covered with white ones.

"Would you rather order something at the take out window or go inside and eat here?" I asked as we were pulling into the parking lot.

"Let's go inside," she said. "You don't see many places like this one anymore, and I would like to soak in the atmosphere."

"Good. You'll enjoy it, and you won't find a better burger than Sunny's Super Special anywhere. Sunny says his secret is sprinkling just the right amount of onion and garlic powder into the hamburger meat, but I think there's more to it than that, and he just won't tell. Oh, and be sure to try the Cajun Fries. They're spicy."

We walked inside and sat across from one another in a corner booth that gave us a good view of traffic on the highway. Our waitress took our drink orders first, a root beer float for me, and a chocolate shake for Myra, and when she returned, we both ordered the Super Special with Cajun Fries for our meal.

As we waited for our food, I asked her how she was feeling, and she said she was not feeling her best, but she thought she would feel better after she had something to eat.

When the waitress placed our dinners on the table, the aroma of the freshly cooked burgers and fries filled the area, and Myra said: "Smells wonderful, doesn't it? Mmmmm. Yum."

"Definitely!" I agreed.

"Are you going to ask the blessing?" she asked.

"Ordinarily I don't ask it out loud, but I will if you like."

"Yes, I think I'd like that," she said.

"Okay, let's bow our heads: We thank you for the blessings of this day and for this meal. We ask that the time we spend together will be time spent in your presence and in your love. Bless this food to our bodies and our bodies to your service. In Christ's name, Amen."

"That was short," she said. "I have a great uncle who's a preacher, and he prays so long the food gets cold while we wait."

"I try to avoid dragging it out too long. Long prayers are best reserved for closets."

"Hey, I remember hearing a sermon about that once," she said. "We're supposed to pray in secret, right?"

"Yes. That's why I don't usually ask the blessing out loud. "

"Oh my gosh, this burger is incredible," she said. "Reminds me of the burgers I used to eat when I was a kid—back before I started feeling guilty for every extra calorie I consumed. Mmm."

"That reminds me. You haven't told me anything about your

childhood. What was it like?"

She stopped chewing for a second, and I could tell that the subject made her at least partly uncomfortable. Had it not been for the burger, I don't think she would have opened up, but good food had put her in a good mood, and she began to talk.

"Let's see? Where do I start?" she asked out loud. "I guess I should start with a thing I don't remember, the accident that happened just before I turned two. According to my mom, my personality was never the same, or at least never consistently the same afterward.

"Mom was driving to the grocery store, and I was strapped in my car seat, but the car seat itself was not fastened in place. At a four way intersection, a truck hit my mom's car. Mom says it was not her fault of course, but I don't guess it really matters.

"The car seat slammed into the dashboard, and the blow knocked me unconscious."

She leaned across the table and lifted her bangs.

"See this scar?" she asked.

I leaned close to her and saw a tiny, pink streak just beneath her scalp line. "Yes, I see it, barely. If you had not called attention to it, I would have never noticed it."

"Well, that's the scar from the accident. Mom was not hurt, but I had to spend three weeks in the hospital, and for half that time I wasn't awake."

"You were in a coma?" I asked.

"Not exactly. I lost consciousness and regained it several times, and twice I stayed out for an entire day. There was a lot of swelling, and I ran fevers too. That's as much as I know about the accident. I've wondered what I would be like if the accident hadn't happened of course, and I've questioned if I am who I am supposed to be, but I've come to terms with the fact that some questions just can't be answered. I am who I am."

"So you didn't have a happy childhood?" I asked.

"Actually, my childhood wasn't so bad. In some ways it was

probably happier than most children's, or maybe I should say some *times* it was happier than most children's. From early on I showed symptoms of more than one major mental disorder, but the symptoms were never consistent, and I took medicine that helped keep me in control of myself."

I didn't know what to say so I nodded, tried to look sympathetic, and moved her to another subject.

"Where did you go to school, and how did you like it?" I asked.

"I loved school, absolutely loved it, school itself, that is. I had trouble forming friendships with the other children as you can imagine, and for that reason I became a bookworm. My teachers knew about my disorders of course, and they were nice to me and tried to get the other children to accept me..."

She stopped talking for a second, and I thought she would cry, but she fought back the urge and continued: "Children are cruel, aren't they? Wait. No, they're not cruel. They're just honest, right? Adults and children think the same things when they see a flaw in someone else, but adults have trained themselves to either ignore the flaw or get away from the person who has it.

"What about you?" she asked. "The first time you saw me starting to get unbalanced, what did you think of me?"

"Do you mean the time I saw you in the grocery store?"

"What? I don't remember seeing you in a grocery store."

"It was Wednesday night. You don't remember making rhymes as you pushed your shopping cart, and I tried to talk to you?"

Her face turned red, and an expression of sad embarrassment engulfed her features.

"I didn't know you had seen me that far gone. I feel so..." She stopped talking again, and an expression of puzzlement replaced her look of embarrassment. "But you went out with me anyway," she resumed. "You knew that I had issues but you went out with me, and you've spent a lot of time with me, and it's been nearly a week now. This is the first time that anyone has..."

She paused again, and I could tell she was lost in thought.

Before she resumed, I asked: "Why did you trust your safe-keeping to me? You barely know me."

She chuckled and said: "Don't take this the wrong way, Rob, but it's obvious you wouldn't hurt a fly. It's in your mannerism, your eyes, and even in your voice. It didn't take half a minute to see that you have a gentle soul and a soft heart."

"Thanks for the compliment," I said. "How could I have taken such kind words the wrong way?"

"Well, you know, men aren't supposed to be gentle, right?"

"Who said that?" I asked.

"Well, nobody said it, but isn't that the way it is?"

"Do you equate gentleness with weakness?" I asked.

"Well, no, I don't guess so," she answered.

"Christ was gentle, and Christians are supposed to be gentle."

"I never heard *that* in church when I was growing up. The preacher used to shout, pound his pulpit, and stomp around like he was angry at everyone there, which when I was small, I thought was pretty fun to watch, but when I got older, it..." She stopped abruptly.

"You just thought about that thing you don't like to talk about that is the reason you stopped going to church, right?"

"Right," she said and wiped her mouth with a paper napkin, took a bite out of her hamburger, and looked out the window as an eighteen wheeler passed on the highway.

"I wouldn't presume to tell you what you should do," I said, "but if whatever happened is bothering you after so much time, maybe you should talk about it. If it's something strictly personal, maybe you should talk about it with Dr. Hernandez, but if it's about a religion, I might understand better than he would."

"Religion can have an extreme effect on people with issues like mine," she said, "especially the religion at the church I attended."

"Let me guess," I said. "The preacher there preached most

of his sermons on hell and judgment. You have some obsessive compulsive tendencies, and you couldn't help thinking bad thoughts sometimes, which made you afraid that you had blasphemed, and you convinced yourself that you were going to hell and nothing could be done about it."

"That's exactly right," she said, "How did you know?"

"You'd be surprised how many people I have counseled over the years who have suffered with the same problem, and most of them have been intelligent, sensitive people, so don't feel bad."

"But I do feel bad," she said. "I believe in God, and I would like to be involved in a church, but I know that I can drive myself crazy thinking too hard about religious subjects, and I'm crazy enough as it is. I wouldn't want to push myself over the edge."

"Don't talk about yourself that way," I said. "You're not crazy, and there is a way to serve God without having to worry that you're going to push yourself over the edge."

"How?" she asked.

"It's pretty easy. If you know you tend to get obsessed with things, just be sure to get obsessed with the right things, the things that will build you up and make you better. Take I John 4:18 for instance: *There is no fear in love, but perfect love casts out fear because fear has torment.* There's a thought to get obsessed with."

"Interesting concept," she said. "I'll have to give it some consideration."

"Was that the reason you stopped going to church?" I asked.

"No, but it relates to it. One Sunday when I was about fifteen the preacher said that if anyone was not sure they would go to Heaven when they died, they should come and kneel at the altar and pray until they were sure. I went forward and kneeled, and my thoughts started going in circles. No matter how much I prayed, I did not feel peace.

"At first, the preacher knelt beside me and prayed. Then he

asked a couple of the ladies in the choir to come and pray with me while he closed the service. They continued to pray with me until everyone else had gone, and the preacher kneeled beside them and prayed too until finally they all just gave up. The choir ladies left, and the preacher told me to stand up and go home. Tears were in my eyes, but I stood and walked outside, and he locked the door behind me. That's when I stopped going to church. I didn't lose my faith in God, but when they gave up trying to help me, I lost my faith in church people."

"Maybe they didn't give up on you," I said. "Maybe they intended to help you someday when you were ready to receive help, but they never got the chance. Sometimes when I start to counsel a person, I realize they are in no frame of mind to receive counseling, and I cut the session short."

"I thought the whole purpose of counseling was to get people in a better frame of mind."

"That's part of the purpose," I said. "But some problems can't be helped by words alone. Sometimes I encourage people to seek medical help. For instance, last year a man came to me because he had begun to have a bad temper, and considering it a spiritual problem, he thought I could help. I told him he should have a doctor give him a physical. He took my advice and learned he had developed high blood pressure. He started taking blood pressure medicine, and his temper went away. His problem was more physical than spiritual. Did the choir ladies and preacher know about the accident when you were a baby?"

"Yes, everyone at my church knew."

"There you go, then. They knew that remaining at the altar would not have helped you, but I'm sure they kept praying for you after they left the church."

"I never really thought about that. Hmm. Maybe they prayed for me, but I don't know."

We finished our supper, put our wrappers, packages, and paper cups in the waste disposal bin, stacked our trays in the slot on the top of the bin, walked outside, got in my car, and drove back to Clegmore.

I stayed at her apartment, and we watched TV until she got sleepy and told me I could go home. I was not expecting to feel any sense of closeness to her so soon - maybe days but probably weeks later - but oddly enough on Tuesday night as I drove home, I got the distinct feeling that somehow our hearts had touched.

Twelve

On Wednesday morning, I took Myra to the library, dropped her off, and drove to the church office. I had to return to the library by three o'clock that afternoon to drive her to her appointment, and I had a lot of work to do so I was trying to get it done as fast as I could when I heard a knock on the church's side door.

I did not wish to be interrupted, but I said, "Come in."

I heard footsteps in the hall, and when the sounds of the footsteps reached my office door, I saw the last person in the world I expected to see: Langston Long.

I stood, walked from behind my desk, extended my hand for a shake and said, "Please come in. What can I do for you, Langston?"

Langston smiled and chuckled. "Reverend, I'm not here for what you can do for me, but what I can do for you."

He was speaking in his best salesman's voice, and I knew better than to take anything he said at face value, but I decided to play along.

"What might that be?"

"It's about Saturday night. I might be able to help you and Miss Findley get the charges changed from resisting arrest to 'illegal U-turn.' In fact, if all goes well and everybody cooperates, the case could be dropped altogether."

"What case? What charges?" I asked.

"Oh come now. I could use the term 'investigation' instead of 'charges' if you prefer, but don't pretend you don't know what I'm talking about," Langston said. "My nephew Warren says the city police got the analysis of the video tape from the forensics lab in Montgomery this morning. It's amazing how much they can figure out with so few clues these days, isn't it?"

I drew in a deep breath and tried to blank the expression on my face.

"You don't have to admit anything," Langston continued. "I'm not here to interrogate you. I'm here to help."

"And how do you propose to do that?" I asked. "And what do you want?"

"Reverend Smith, you insult me. I'm not here to blackmail you. Blackmail is as illegal as resisting arrest and reckless endangerment. It's not a quid pro quo I'm offering. I'm only offering to do you a favor. Now, I can't say I wouldn't be happy if you dropped your opposition to the good things I'm trying to do for this city, but that would be your decision."

I felt cornered and helpless. Langston seemed so full of confidence that I could not help taking him seriously, but then he had been a professional salesman for his entire life. If he were bluffing, I wouldn't be able to tell the difference.

"Would you give me some time to think it over?" I asked.

"Of course. Take the rest of the day. I understand that you have something personal at stake in all this so when you talk to Miss Findley, you can even let her think that you're pulling the strings if you like. I don't care who she credits for helping her so long as *you* know the truth."

"When should I give you an answer?"

"How about tomorrow by lunch time? I usually have lunch at The Sweet Shop. Why don't you join me?"

When I returned to the library, Myra asked me what was wrong, but since I did not want to upset her before her appointment, I did not tell her.

"Oh, it's nothing," I said. "Are you ready?"

"I'm not excited about having to go, but I'm as ready as

I'll ever be."

Except for sections that pose specific health risks, pastors are given twenty-four hour access to all areas in the Clegmore Hospital, so when Myra was called back for the initial procedures leading to her exam, I stepped through the door and strolled about the halls until I saw Dr. Hernandez. He was standing at the end of a long corridor. He was facing a window, and his back was to me, but I recognized him by his dark complexion and short, close-cropped white hair.

I approached him slowly: "Dr. Hernandez, I'm glad I bumped into you. You're just the man I need to talk to."

"Yes?" he asked as he turned around and without raising his eyes to greet me made notes on the papers on his clipboard.

"There's a member of my church who may need to see you. He has a problem with shyness. Well, not exactly. It's only in some circumstances."

"What situations? Crowds? Large social gatherings? Very common thing, you know, and not usually the sort of thing that requires a psychiatrist."

"Actually, no. He can handle crowds and large social gatherings with no difficulty. His problem is talking one-on-one to certain people."

"What people?" he asked, lifting his eyes and looking me over.

I leaned close to him: "Beautiful women. He gets shy around beautiful women."

Dr. Hernandez laughed out loud. "Ha! That's no problem for a psychiatrist. It's hardly even a problem for a psychologist. Your friend should save his time and money and buy a self help book or just settle for dating ugly women. They need love too, you know."

He laughed out loud again, patted my shoulder, and walked down the hall.

I felt silly, and for a few seconds, I stood and looked out the window. Then I took a deep breath, sighed, and made my routine hospital rounds while I waited for Myra to complete her appointment. As I walked around the hospital, I kept glancing at my watch, and when I thought it was almost time for Myra's appointment to end, I went and sat in the outpatient care lobby and started reading a two month old issue of *Modern Maturity*.

A few minutes later, a nurse opened the door, and Myra entered the lobby.

"Well?" I asked.

"Come on," she said. "I'll tell you about it while we walk to the car."

I put the magazine down and walked beside her.

"You were right about Dr. Hernandez. He made me feel comfortable. He seems like a nice man."

"Yes, he is nice and honest too," I said. "What did he tell you?"

"He said that since the changes I've experienced in the past week are most likely stress related I will get better as I settle into my new job. His only advice was that I should start exercising in the afternoons."

"He didn't increase the dosage of your medicine?"

"No. He said he would increase my dosage only as a last resort. That's good news. I hate taking pills."

Myra looked genuinely happy, and I did not wish to bring her down, but I had to tell her about Langston's visit.

On the drive back to the library, I told her everything that Langston had told me, and her mood shifted from jubilant to pensive. I thought she was weighing her options, but when we reached the library she rushed inside and began searching the card catalogue as if the entire matter rested on whatever she expected to find.

"What are you looking for?" I asked.

"If you do what he says, he wins, and the library loses. If you don't, they'll come after me, and if they prove their case, I lose, you lose, and the library loses. I could turn myself in of course, but since this is a critical time, if I do, it'll provide the ammunition he needs, and the library loses. If everything he said was true, no matter what happens, he wins so he wouldn't have come to you this morning unless they had a weak case. Can't you see it? They don't have a strong case, Rob, or at least they don't yet. It's obvious they're waiting for something to happen. Come on. Follow me."

I followed her to the non-fiction section where she pulled a large book titled *An Introduction to Forensic Science.*

She placed the book on a study table, paused to read the table of contents, and turned to chapter nineteen: *Automobiles.*

I read over her shoulder, and I felt quite astonished because I never realized how much information investigators gather from tire prints. One page explained various techniques for identifying vehicles, and we read every detail.

"You say I covered the tag pretty thoroughly with mud, right?" she asked.

"Right," I said.

"So their only chance of proving it was my car would be by some other identifier, right?"

"Right," I agreed.

"And since we stayed on paved roads, they can't trace the tires, right?"

"Well, you did peel out once or twice," I said.

"But that would be their only identifier other than the video, right?"

"Yes, right." I said.

"Let's look up *video,*" she said as she flipped to the chapter on surveillance techniques.

She read for a few minutes, handed me the book, pointed to a particular paragraph and asked, "Well, what do you think?"

"I think Langston is bluffing," I said. "The car was dark inside and the lights were bright outside and according to this, there's no way they could have gotten a clear shot of either of us. I doubt there really is a video."

"Let's look it up," she said.

In the local records department, she found copies of the city police budget for the past fifteen years. The library wasn't the only institution behind the times. There was no record of video cameras having ever been installed.

"He's definitely bluffing, but even so I think he has an ulterior motive," she said. "If he is as you have described him, he's the sort who always thinks three moves ahead."

"Meaning?"

"He expects that you could figure out he's bluffing, but having figured it out, you could make matters worse than they were."

"How?"

"By getting in a hurry and doing something stupid like trying to destroy what little evidence exists—the tires on my car."

"Well, well, Miss Librarian, you have located all the pertinent information. What do we do now?"

"Something his type would never expect," she said. "I'm turning myself in."

"Are you kidding? You can't do that. Not in this town. That would be the end of you in this town."

"I'm not turning myself in to anyone in this town. I'm calling state headquarters. If Langston knew about Saturday night, his nephew or someone on the force told him, and the implications of that are pretty big."

Thirteen

After she locked up, we got in my car, and I asked: "So, where would you like to eat? We only have an hour before church starts."

"I want you to know that you don't have to watch me anymore, Rob. I was already feeling better before I saw Dr. Hernandez, and after speaking with him, I feel sure that I'm going to be able to stabilize myself."

"Does that mean you won't be going to church tonight?"

"Actually, no, I want to go to your church. I just want you to know that I'm going because I want to, not because I have to. Over the past three days, I've been thinking about my faith, and I need to get back to it. I thank you for that.

"You make me believe that God is all about mercy. It's not so much the things you've said as it is the kindness you've shown, really. I feel like you look past... you know... you look past stuff that other guys haven't been able to look past, and you focus on the better side of me."

I didn't know what to say. My shy side took over, and I felt my face turn red.

We ate at Grandma's Kitchen, and after supper we hurried to the church. Word had gotten around that I was seeing someone so the congregation was larger than usual that evening. When Myra and I arrived together, we satisfied their curiosity. Yes, I was seeing someone.

The Bible study went well, and afterward I drove her to her apartment and said goodnight for the evening. She wanted me to be with her the next morning when the detective came, so to be sure I would be wide awake, I went home and got in bed early.

That night I dreamt the strangest dream. I suddenly found myself in a great ballroom, and before I had time to ask where or why, I saw Myra—actually two Myras. I saw Myra Findley, the strong, beautiful librarian and Myra Findley, the frail human being. The two Myras were dressed in gorgeous, pink silk dresses, and they were dancing with gentlemen wearing tuxedos.

At first I did not recognize the gentlemen, but as they drew close I saw that each one was *me*. My shy, insecure self was dancing with Myra's strong self, and my confident, outspoken self was dancing with her weak self. The two gentlemen always kept their backs to each other.

The dream ended abruptly. It was a vivid dream, and although it had no plot, it remained with me when I woke up and filled my mind as I drove to the library to meet with Myra and the detective.

When I got there, the detective had not arrived. Myra had arrived, but she had not yet opened the library for patrons. I knocked on the library's side door, and she opened for me. I saw immediately that she was in her best state, and for her sake, I was glad for it.

While we waited for the detective, she made some coffee and asked if I wanted a cup. I accepted the coffee, and as we chatted, the dream kept going through my mind. I realized that despite all the progress we had made in relating to one another, my shy side kept coming to the surface in the face of her most beautiful side. What a sad condition in which I found myself, perhaps as sad as Myra's. I was as divided as a person could be.

Like a lightning bolt, an answer came. The fact that the two Roberts in the dream had their backs to each other was the key to understanding what my subconscious was telling me. I had to integrate the two sides of me. I had to let each side see the other side.

Right then and there as Myra was speaking and my shy side

was ruling my behavior, I forced myself to think about my other side. I reminded myself that I could address large crowds without feeling nervous and that large crowds responded positively to my addressing them. I forced my shy side to have a good look at my bold side, but at the same time, I forced my bold side to recognize the value of my sensitivity and gentleness.

In short, I forced each side of myself to view the opposite side in a good light, and I felt myself melting together and becoming whole as I did so. I knew getting to a better place would take much work, but I believed I was off to a good start.

Myra snapped her fingers in front of my face and said, "Rob, are you okay?"

"Huh?"

"Are you there? You look like you're in a trance. Snap out of it. The detective just pulled into the parking lot."

"Oh, I was just thinking. Never mind. I'll go and let him in."

The detective, a young man with salt and pepper hair, introduced himself as Lieutenant Eric McKenzie, and we shook hands. We went to Myra's office, and she began her confession by showing him her prescription medicine.

She went on to tell him the whole story, and when she finished he said: "I'm not going to charge you. There's little or no evidence, and even if a prosecutor could prove the case, your medical condition would get you off. However, I could use your help, Mr. Smith."

"My help? Sure, whatever you need."

"Would you be willing to testify against Langston Long's nephew Warren?"

"Yes, but surely he's not going to have charges brought against him over something so small? He only passed along information, and it would be my word against Langston's word."

"Oh no. This is a minor thing, but a telling one. Dirtiness always comes out in more ways than one. We've been investigating him for six months now for his role in trafficking drugs with a relative of his who runs a local pawnshop. We're closing in, and we hope to get them both at the same time, probably in the next two weeks. We think Langston is involved too, but we're not sure how. Maybe we could charge him with attempted blackmail."

"An old guy like Langston trafficking drugs? No way," I said.

Lieutenant McKenzie laughed, "We busted an eighty-one year old woman two weeks ago. She was rich and had a big pension from her husband too, but I guess she needed a little more."

The detective asked us to say nothing to anyone about the investigation, and we agreed to keep quiet. Myra had been right. Her honesty in confessing had placed the library out of harm's way. Of course there would always be the detective's report, but there are thousands of reports filed every day and since no charges were being filed, it would probably never be read.

When the detective left, Myra returned to the front desk, and I drove to the church office. My thoughts drifted back to the dream, and I explored what I thought of as my bold side. I considered that my boldness could have been a cover for underlying weaknesses. Some people speak loud not because they are brave but because they fear their voice is not significant. Was I one of those people?

Before I answered, I reminded myself that too much introspection is self-destructive. I purposed to make the two sides of myself see the other and left it at that.

At lunchtime, I met Langston at the Sweet Shop. He rose to greet me, told his friends he would be back, and walked across the room.

"Let's get a booth," he said. "I'm glad you came."

"I'm not here to eat," I said. "I just wanted to let you know I won't be dropping my petition."

For a few seconds Langston said nothing. Then he snorted, cleared his throat, and said: "Well, I guess I'll go eat with my friends." He knew I had called his bluff, and anything else he said would have only lost him more face. He stood and walked across the room, and I left for lunch at Grandma's Kitchen.

When Ben knows a big secret, an expression comes to his face like that a child wears when he has seen his Christmas presents before Christmas morning. I guess it's a reporter thing. Ben was wearing that expression when I walked into the restaurant and he motioned me over to his table.

"Rob, you're never going to believe this. A detective from state headquarters stopped by this morning. He wants the paper to work with him on an investigation. He says you're in on this thing, but we're not supposed to talk about it."

"Good. Let's not talk about it. You-know-who is no longer a threat, but my problems aren't over. Let me ask you something, Ben. You got married right out of high school, and it's worked. How does something like that happen? How does it work? Explain it to me. I'm starting something new, and I don't know how."

"That's easy," Ben said. "You don't ask how it works. You don't ask how it happened or what's going to happen. You just go with it. You don't dwell on the past, and you don't worry about the future. Just go with it."

"Just go with it, huh?"

"Yup, it's pretty simple. Usually the more you analyze the less it works."

There was nothing more to say about that so we changed the subject to sports and talked about baseball as we ate. After lunch, I made my usual rounds at the hospital, went back to the office, and wrote a couple of best wishes cards. I kept my mind occupied with chores. I knew what I wanted to say to Myra, but I did not want to think about how I was going to say it. When the time came, I wanted to speak from my heart. I wanted both sides of my personality to do the speaking at once.

The time came after work. She invited me over to her apartment for a supper of sandwiches, chips, and soft drinks. When we finished eating she handed me the remote control to find something interesting on TV, but I did not turn on the set.

Instead, I said: "Myra, there are thousands of towns in this country just like this one and thousands of guys just like me, but of all the towns, I'm glad you moved to this one, and of all the guys, I'm glad I was the one who got to meet you. The first time I saw you, I saw the greatest beauty I had ever beheld! In my eyes, you have grown even more beautiful since then, but I do not mean to say too much too soon. I only want one thing right now: All I want is to know everything about you. You amaze me."

For what seemed like a lifetime, there was an uncomfortable silence. Then Myra smiled and tears came to her eyes. She leaned toward me as if she wanted to be hugged, and I reached out to hug her.

Fourteen

That weekend the state police busted Langston's cousin and nephew. They both confessed and in so doing, they implicated Langston. So as not to establish a pattern, they had been using cars from his lot to transport drugs. A big story ran on the front page of the *Progressive*, and that was the end of the library's troubles.

A week later, Myra and I attended the annual Valentine's Banquet together, and everyone said we made a nice couple. I knew they were being more than kind to me by saying such a thing, and I thanked everyone profusely.

That was a year ago today. Six months after we met, I asked the big question, and she said yes.

Today is Valentine's Day, a perfect day for a wedding.

It all worked out, and I'm still surprised. At my age, I never thought anything like this would, but you know what they say: You never can tell.

Now what I'm about to say is going to sound preachy, and I know you shouldn't end a story this way, but hey, I'm a preacher, so why not?

We've all got our good and bad sides. If you want to find love and joy in this lifetime you've got to live by mercy. Focus on the best in people and ignore all the bad that you can ignore. It's really that simple.

Do not miss:

The Wisdom of Shepherds

the masterpiece by Rhett Ellis

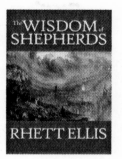

T*he Wisdom of Shepherds* is the story of Old Caleb the shepherd. One winter he returns to the crumbling cottage he has used for shelter for fifty years and hears a strange voice singing a strange song. He fears that the mysterious singer has unearthed the secret thing he buried beneath the cottage when he was a young man. He knocks on the cottage door, and a woman with red hair opens it.

What follows is a humorous, good-natured yarn full of powerful emotion, wisdom, and fun.

Printed in the United States
22620LVS00001B/157-162